PLUMP *Jane*

PLUMP JANE

PLUMP PLAYWRIGHT ACT I

At night, scatter-brained, eccentric Jane Myerson pours her soul into her romance novels writing as J.J. Cox. During the day, she's a lonely woman hiding behind her plump backside.

Max Reynolds is a fitness YouTube star plagued by a string of unhappy relationships, the last ending in divorce. Tired of hiding his pain behind a smile, he spots Jane in dire need of his expertise.

With her book tour four months away, Jane accepts Max's offer to tone. But the poor man is unprepared for her chaotic life, that of mugger-tackling and bush-diving. She's certain he could never see her in a romantic light.

Day-by-day, she falls for him. Dare she reveal she's J.J. and lose her chance at happiness?

PLUMP JANE

Plump Playwright Act I

by Sevannah Storm

Also by Sevannah Storm

The Blood of Legends Series

The Huntress

The Healer

*

The Gifting Series

Soul Forged

Fate Forged

Sun Forged

War Forged

Star Forged

Shadow Forged

Earth Forged

Lust Forged

Fire Forged

*

The Qaldreth Warriors

Sol Survivor

Dark Survivor (Coming soon)

*

The Space Hunter Chronicles

The Shikari

The Justisaar

*

Inkounter Series

Inkoded

*

Standalones

Xiaxan Fox

Ire of Silver

The Crucible of the Eternal

*

Plump Playwright Series

Plump Jane

Seducing Amelia

Loving Finley

Keeping Tessa

Kissing Navy

Chapter One

ArdentMan

☆☆☆☆☆ I'm so addicted!
Reviewed on January 12, 2018
Verified Purchase

Yet another to reread and pine over. I love J.J. Cox
and her writing style. This one has found a
permanent spot on my night stand and in my heart.
XOXO

JANE CRUSHED THE LAMINATED card to her chest, smearing mustard over it from the blob she dribbled earlier. She sighed, then used a paper towel to clean it before pressing her lips to the warm plastic, uncaring about the stain on her summer dress. ArdentMan was one of her pseudonym's biggest fans. He commented days after each book release, and his responses were so passionate that she printed and laminated his reviews.

Tipping her face to the sunlight, she basked in its warmth, content to spread her legs on the picnic blanket. A half-empty bottle of diet soda, a mangled chocolate wrapper, and J.J. Cox's new novel rested beside her. She had it printed to do a final read-through before giving the publishers the go-ahead.

Trevor, her day-job boss, hadn't called her since nine this morning, and she didn't expect him to while he was on a flight to Uruguay.

She grimaced, scooped up the book, and laid down, flicking her sunglasses into place. Having spent weeks editing the latest saga in her Crossroads Biker series, she didn't want to read it. She longed to discover a new author whose novels inspired her and gave her sexy vibes when she read their words.

Tugging her dress down to hide her plump thighs she flashed the poor park visitors, she wiggled her backside, trying to find a comfortable spot. Nope, something rocklike lay beneath her blanket, and she didn't have the energy to remove it.

"Oh, fudgeknuckles." She thumped the book down, and hoisted herself across, trapping the wrapper under her ass, and spiraling the bottle outward. Trying to stop it from rolling downhill toward the pond, she lunged for it. The bottle evaded her outstretched hand as it bounced, leaped, and hit someone on their sneaker.

Closing her eyes, she drew in a steady breath. She hadn't wanted to speak to anyone, never did, which was why her assistant position to a traveling executive was perfect. Now she would have to get off her ass and interact, thanking them for thwarting her soda's bid for freedom.

"Is this yours, miss?" A deep voice rippled along her senses; seductive, husky, promising sweaty nights of unabashed passion, of which she had little knowledge.

J.J. Cox did, and perhaps in an alternative universe, her pseudonym would be the one sitting in a park, and Jane would be the main character in one of her sexually explicit novels.

"Yes, thank you." Grateful for her sunglasses, she raised her gaze to the man standing at the edge of her blanket. Her breath snagged as she lingered on his bulging calves, sculpted thigh muscles, up past his jogging shorts to the Adonis belt peeking out. A sweat-drenched tank accentuated a barrel chest and mile-wide shoulders.

Her heart fluttered, and she dipped her face to hide how much he flustered her. He shifted. Ice slid down her spine at the thought that he might step onto her blanket and breach her safe zone.

He dropped to his haunches beside her bringing blond curls and gray eyes into her line of sight. Blue jelly babies, he was a stunner. His angled jaw and dimpled chin tempted her to touch him, and if that wasn't enough, those plump lips pulled up at the corner. Oh, miracle of Moses, don't smile, she couldn't take it.

"Is that a J.J. Cox?"

His question stumped her, and she scanned the blanket for the discarded book. "I ARC for her." The lie slipped from her tongue like a hot spoon through double-chocolate chip ice cream.

"Wow, I'd love to receive an advanced copy."

She lifted her sunglasses to meet his gaze. He knew what an ARC was. She grinned. "I'm impressed. I usually have to explain it, the process behind it, and how crucial advanced readers are for the author." Her focus shifted to the sweat dewing his forehead and trickling down his temple. His skin looked like soft toffee, the kind she sucked off each fingertip.

He chuckled, formed a full smile, and exploded Jane's heartbeat into a gallop a jockey would have been proud of. She shivered and ran her hands along her forearms, hoping to calm the goosebumps.

"How did you get on the list? Where can I apply?" he asked.

She didn't expect men to love her stories, but the demographics showed their interest was climbing. "Here, take this one." Anything for him to leave, she thrust the book at him. Doctors believed oxygen was necessary for life, but the way her ribs squeezed her lungs, she would either expire on the spot or prove them wrong.

"Are you sure?" He hesitated, then his long fingers wrapped around the book, brushing hers.

She yelped, yanking her hand back. "Sorry, static." Being her overdramatic self, she held her stinging fingers to her lips, testing the temperature of her burned skin. For a moment there, she had hoped it wasn't static but that amazing chemistry she drenched her novels with. Silly her. That sort of connection didn't exist in real life, but alas, she still hoped.

"I'm Max, and if you can get me on the ARC list, I'd appreciate it." He offered his card, while she admired his shorts, wondering where he had pulled it from. No, she didn't linger on his package, just the angles of his hips, the way the fabric pulled across his tight ass. Then his package, but a glance nothing more. Scouts' honor.

Her fingers trembled as she pinched the card between forefinger and thumb. When no lightning struck her, she released her pent-up breath in a whoosh. Another spark would have carried her hope through the next round of novels.

"I'm a personal fitness trainer." He ran an appraising eye over her sprawled body, and something intense darkened his eyes. "Your curves are beautiful, but I'd love to work with you *if* you want to tone." The tip of his tongue dipped his upper lip. "Free of charge, of course..." He arched a brow, waiting for her name.

He liked her curves? She gaped, torn between disbelief at his blatant interest, and dismay at the mention of her...curves.

"Jane." Whoever said her name wasn't her, because that voice sounded raspy, flustered, and drenched with need. So were her thighs, and she should dismiss her reaction to this man by stating it was a hot spring day. Instant attraction was the stuff of novels.

"Do you have a bicycle?" His question floored her, and she stared at him in a daze. "One with wheels, not a clotheshorse?"

"It's ancient." Somewhere in the back of her garage was Mom's bicycle. Ancient was an understatement.

"Gym clothes?" He ran his thumb across the fabric gathered at her cleavage and licked the mustard off it. His nostrils flared, and he groaned. The gravel sound sent her minding-their-own business-hormones spiraling, and the sweet nectar of lust slammed into her. "They do make the best hot dogs here."

She trembled, heat bursting across her cheeks and rampaging down to her tingling skin he had touched a moment ago. She couldn't believe he had done that. What if it wasn't mustard? She was being an idiot, and rightly so. What other condiment was yellow?

"Why did you do that?" She winced, having not meant to ask him.

He smiled, unrepentant, ran his gaze over her heaving bosom, and lingered on her lips. "I couldn't resist."

"What if it wasn't mustard? What if I wasn't clean? Like I was some sort of unhygienic slob?"

First, this man spoke to her. That spun her mind from scenario to disbelief faster than a slingshot. Second, she should be pissed. He might as well have licked her chest. The explosion of goosebumps snatched her breath. *Wow, okay, don't go there, Jane.*

He threw back his head and laughed. The richness of it was so unexpected, it summoned a smile.

"The hotdog wrapper suggested the yellow smear was a condiment." He gestured to the scrunched ball of paper on the edges of her picnic blanket. "And," he caught up a stray curl, "your hair is damp." Rubbing the strands between his fingers, he met her gaze with an arched brow. "So?"

Oh, shit. He had asked her a question. She chewed on her lip and sifted through her recent memories. Shaking her head dragged her hair from his hand. "No to the gym clothes."

He frowned. "What do you wear when you exercise?"

Nightmares of lying on a towel in her bedroom trying to do yoga had her grimacing.

"Um, my birthday suit?" She gasped and jumped up, throwing items into her bag.

Why had she said that? He flustered her, that's for sure, and she would blame him if the government decided to question her. A scenario played out in her mind, one of the hazards of being a writer. Handcuffed to the chair, she would spill the beans before the first nipple clamp. *I was powerless against his spicy, intoxicating, addictive scent, sir. Bottle that, see if it will work on female spies.* She snorted at missing her calling in espionage.

"I'll be at the Rose Mall tomorrow at nine. Meet me there, and we'll get what you need." He had given her more space, but it wasn't enough. She could still draw in a deep breath and fill her lungs with his brain-numbing cologne.

Meet him? Why? "I don't need to exercise, Max. I'm fine as I am." She yanked the blanket off the ground, then tossed it over one shoulder, uncaring that she raised a small dust cloud. Her cell phone rang, and she juggled the items to yank it out of the bag.

"Jane speaking." She hadn't checked who the caller was, but the slight lull implied long distance.

"Jane, dearest, glad I caught you." Her agent, Wendy Dumont, rattled on expecting to have a moment of Jane's time.

Max's attention remained on her face as if she hadn't rebuffed his suggestion. Fitness wasn't her thing, and never would be. One glance, okay make that a linger, told her how much health mattered to him.

"So, the book tour is in four months. I'll make all the arrangements from my side, but expect to spend three weeks on the road." Wendy laughed. "I can't wait to meet you in person, Jane."

"What?" Jane dragged her gaze from the Greek god standing before her.

"The tour's in your contract, sugar. Don't bother trying to wiggle your way out of it."

"But—" Ice and lava took turns to lambaste her face, and she smothered a sob. Wendy had hung up, leaving Jane to stare at the phone, horror squeezing her vision until black circled it. She dropped her things as her world spun.

Max caught her, cupping her elbows to keep her upright. "Whoa, Jane, breathe."

"Four months," she said, tugging herself out of his arms.

She kneeled then sprawled onto the grass, uncaring that she looked like a beached walrus in a summer dress. When dizziness struck, she had to go horizontal as soon as possible. No way was she accepting the blame for seismic activity if she hit the ground. Twenty pounds overweight meant she exaggerated, then again she was lying to herself. Maybe, thirty? Surely not forty pounds?

"Are you all right?" Max leaned over her, his face above hers, and for a moment, as the sun haloed his golden locks, she thought Gabriel himself had come down from heaven. "Bad news?"

She flapped her mouth in shock. How to explain that she had a J.J. Cox book tour, and she dreaded it to the very marrow of her thick bones. "A...work function I can't get out of."

His touch burned where he gripped her waist, and before she could warn him that chiropractic appointments were expensive, he hoisted her off the ground.

She blinked, finding herself standing, her fingers embedded in his massive biceps. Her mouth parted on a "wow."

"What's so bad about a work function?" With a gentle touch, he tugged bits of grass out of her hair.

"I'm a recluse. This is it for me." She gestured to the park. "Here, and home."

"Well, if we work toward the function, maybe you'll feel more prepared." He wrapped his fingers around her upper arm, as if to steady her. "Nine at the Rose Mall, Jane." He booped her nose with his fingertip. "Don't keep me waiting."

She watched him jog off, his long strides covering the distance to the parking lot. Fudgeknuckles, what the hell had just happened? It sounded like a date, but she knew better. He hoped to inspire in her the love of exercise when chocolates, writing, and her male characters owned all the acreage of her heart. Not even for the Adonis that he was would she grant exercise a square foot of prime real estate.

Sweat trickled between her breasts, and she grimaced, bending to collect her things. He did have a point though. Four months to the book tour, and not going meant violating her contract. What if he could help her tone a little? If he could boost her self-confidence?

It would be lovely to climb stairs without sounding like an asthmatic cat. Exercising meant getting her out of the house, away from Mom, who had it in mind to test out her newfound porn star skills on unsuspecting geriatrics.

Dumping everything into the boot of her car, she squeezed herself behind the wheel. Voluptuous and short meant her breasts could steer. She started the engine, and paused, gathering her hair into a ponytail.

Between now and nine tomorrow, she expected to change her mind about meeting Max at least a dozen times. She would bet her last Lindt ball, he wouldn't be seeing her.

Chapter Two

Max cursed, calling himself all kinds of a fool. How low had he fallen to accost a plump woman at the park? Her huffing and grunting as she tried to find a comfortable spot had drawn his attention, along with the mass of brown hair swaying around her. When her soda bottle had struck his foot, he succumbed to the temptation and approached her.

Solidifying his strange need to talk to her was J.J. Cox's new book now resting on his passenger seat. Excitement at an evening spent reading warred with the hope that Jane would show up tomorrow. If she didn't, he could see himself loitering in the park, waiting for her.

Why his interest? Her expressions had said as much, as if she distrusted his motives. He scowled, gripping and releasing his steering wheel. She needed him, her unhealthy choice of meals clear with the sting of mustard on his tongue. Helping her would heal him, the broken, unloved part of his soul. That was his angle, his last-ditch attempt to maintain his sanity.

Jane. Her name suited her—mousy hair and big brown eyes in a pale face scattered with freckles. Nothing remarkable, yet that didn't explain the connection between them. Static, she had said, but he knew better. Energy charged through his veins, and he had to admit, it had been years since he felt this alive.

He parked the car in his garage, snatching the book before taking the steps two at a time to the front door. Liking that he had flustered her, he smiled. Then again, what had made him run his thumb along her cleavage? Her breasts had threatened to break free from the top of her dress, and the bright yellow smear had drawn his gaze too many times to count. She glowed with health, and the heat of her skin had saturated his thumb. Madness had claimed him, although the mustard had tasted good. He didn't eat processed meats anymore nor did he drench his food in colorants.

She did, along with the soda and the candy wrapper stuck to her dress. Her diet would have to change first. He chuckled, closing the door behind him. Despite being a self-proclaimed recluse, she would argue with him, gathering her courage around her. He would be lying if he didn't admit he looked forward to it.

Something about her said eccentric, and he needed that, a change from his usual clientele. Bored housewives hoping to bone their trainer? Jane was far from it.

His cock twitched, and he frowned. Would he do her if he could? He nodded. Draped across her blanket, she had looked like an exotic Rubenesque woman, soft, enticing with a natural sensuality in her movements. He wouldn't pursue her though; it was why he dated fitness fanatics. Max Reynolds, YouTube fitness guru, couldn't date a plump woman, no matter how much he wanted her.

He undressed and stepped into the shower, rinsing off the sweat and dust from his jog. His bathroom door opened, and he twisted his body, hiding his privates.

Growling, he flicked a glare at his sister through the fogged glass. "Abby, not in here."

She harrumphed and lowered the toilet seat before slumping onto it. "I had a shitty day at school."

"Language," he said, but washing his face drowned out his admonishment. "Fine, we can order in. Just do it instead of harassing me."

"Nope, I need more than a chicken wrap. I want chocolate smeared across my face, and my fingertips drenched in colorants."

He sighed. At fourteen, his sister exhausted him. Fifteen years her senior, he shouldn't have connected with her considering such a large age gap. But when a freak boating accident took their parents, he became her guardian and surrogate father. Connection was a given.

Sensing she wouldn't leave him alone unless he caved, he slid the door open and flicked water at her before smiling. "If you leave me alone for five minutes, I'll unlock the freezer."

A whoop and the slamming of the door had him resting his forehead on the cold tiles. He loved her. He did. Emily hadn't been able to deal with Abby as part of the package.

From single to married, and a mother to a teenager? Max shook his head. It was why he was a divorcee at thirty. Singlehood loomed until Abby went off to college.

Fitness mattered to him. He couldn't control life or death nor could he remove the sadness that had consumed Abby for two years after the accident. But he could control his body, what he fed it, and when posting his fitness tips on YouTube turned into a career, he pursued the necessary qualifications.

His thoughts returned to Jane. She challenged him, gave him something to focus on other than his broken heart and empty bed. After toweling himself dry, he pulled on yoga pants and a tank.

Abby waited in the kitchen, spoon in hand, leaning her hip against the padlocked freezer. He bought tubs of homemade ice cream filled with fruit, and double-cream dairy—the good kind.

"You'll eat dinner without complaint?" He arched a brow then chuckled, sliding the numbers into the lock. It clicked, and she gasped, bouncing on her toes.

Max stepped back, granting her access, and she dived into the freezer, pulling out the last dark-chocolate tub. He made a note on the fridge to order more. She could have whatever she wanted for lunch at school since he couldn't control her choices. At home, she ate well.

"Planning on sharing?" He pulled a spoon out of the drawer, but she darted around the island, laughing around spoonfuls of ice cream. Max chose a tub at random, locked the freezer, and grabbed Jane's J.J. Cox. He sunk into his couch and popped the lid off the tub.

"This looks new." Abby tapped the end of the spoon on the book before pointing at his bookshelf.

Seven J.J. Cox books took center stage on the top shelf, their spines scarred from too many rereads, and the pages gaping from the dog-eared corners. He meant to replace them, but he had underlined his favorite passages, and with the number of bookmarks he needed, he had to resort to dog-earing the pages, instead.

"From my new client, Jane." He clenched his jaw. Since he had bulldozed the poor woman, it wouldn't surprise him if she stood him up tomorrow. Free of charge? He didn't need her money, but now that he replayed their conversation, he had implied he wanted to date her.

He closed his eyes as he slipped a spoonful of strawberries and cream into his mouth. Her heaving bosom, her nibbling on her plump bottom lip, the way her breath hitched and her gaze had lingered on parts of his anatomy? Any reader of J.J. Cox would recognize the symptoms.

He grinned. To make an impact in her life, he would use her attraction to him. When he was done with her, she wouldn't hide behind voluminous, unflattering dresses. She would show off those divine curves.

He hoped she showed up tomorrow since he was basing his future happiness on her. Desperation gripped him, and he tightened his fingers around the spoon. If she didn't show, what would he do? Who would help him find himself again, the man he had been in his early twenties? The younger Max who hadn't feared to love or to pursue what he wanted?

That man was missing, and for some strange reason, Max had chosen Jane to save him.

Chapter Three

"MOM," JANE CRIED OUT, "what did I say about bringing these men home? For someone who watches an excessive amount of crime shows, you have no sense of self-preservation."

As usual, Mom ignored her, flittering around the kitchen on the last dregs of sexual euphoria. She wore a leopard-print negligee that covered nothing, humming to herself as she scooped cream into her coffee.

Jane sighed and stared at the wall clock. In half an hour, she'll have stood up the Adonis. Guilt struck true, twisting a knife in her heart. She focused on her coffee, cycling through her breathing exercises as she fought the urge to dive into her car.

"Stan was amazing last night. He might be a keeper." Mom resumed humming, ignoring Jane, who mouthed 'Stan.'

She smothered a giggle, placing Stan as her new male character.

Stanley gathered Felicity in his warm embrace and pressed a kiss to her quivering lips.

She gasped. "Oh, Stanley, how handsome you are."

Jane shook her head. The chance of naming her main character Stan was like finding ice cream in hell—a two percent probability.

"...such stamina, Jane-dear."

Jane slammed her mug down and cupped her ears. Miracle of Moses, not another recap of the previous night's antics. Her stomach churned, and the hope of bacon abandoned her to her suffering.

Mom put her mug down and glared. "You write erotica, for pity's sake. Even a woman my age has needs."

Jane lowered her hands, scowling at her unsupportive mother who lived in *her* house, paid by *her* erotic fantasies. "I write romance with erotic elements, there's a difference."

Mom rolled her eyes in a classic "whatever." Jane huffed. It was like living with a teenager.

"Well, someone in this house has to live out their fantasies." Mom tightened her pointless gown around her taut figure. She looked amazing for her age, but Jane wouldn't admit that to her.

"Mine earns an income, Mom."

"You live in a dream world, Jane. Live a little, meet a man, experience a real orgasm for once." Mom ran her gaze over Jane, and she shifted on her stool. "Using your toys isn't exercise, dear."

Jane pinched her lips. She knew what orgasms felt like, self-imposed, of course. "Losing ten pounds will magic a man into my life?" One who would tolerate her seclusion and long working hours? She doubted it.

"Try thirty."

Jane flinched. She grabbed her bag, fluffed her hair, and slipped her car keys off the hook.

"You can't run away from the truth, Jane-dear."

"I'm not...running." Jane gritted her teeth. "I have an appointment with a personal trainer." She dug out Max's card and slammed it onto the counter. Ninety-eight point seven percent of her body, her mind included, reeled from her decision that she would meet him.

Yanking open the door, she stomped to her car, praying she hit traffic. If she delayed, he might grow impatient, freeing her from this. Then again, for the next four months, she would have to pretend to meet him, pretend to diet, and wash brand-new and unused gym clothes so her mother wouldn't suspect a thing.

Speeding and taking corners way too fast shot bolts of adrenaline through Jane as she wrestled with her conscience. It would be easier to give in and let Max help her than lie to her mom.

She pulled into the mall's parking lot, gripping the steering wheel until the fake leather bit into her palms. The trip had taken her fifteen minutes. A hysterical giggle rose to choke her, but she tamped it down. The panic-laced smile clung to her lips, and the reflection in the mirror said she had gone feral.

She wore an empire-style dress, cinched under her breasts thrusting them upward and beyond. Since she had no intention of meeting him, she hadn't dressed in a flattering way. Her brown hair tumbled down her back, needing a trim. So did her eyebrows, which had entered a camouflage-yourself-as-a-caterpillar contest.

Grumbling about the state of her life and those tormenting her, she applied what she had in the car. Eyeliner, mascara, bright pink lipstick, and a quick plucking of the caterpillars. With ten minutes to go, she fluffed her hair and climbed out, dragging her monstrous bag behind her.

He had said to meet her, but he hadn't said where. The sporting warehouse was somewhere in the building as per their advertising board. Her knowledge of the mall centered around the coffee shops, chocolate delicatessen, and bookstores. Except for the adult store, she didn't deviate from her haunts.

She strode to the information desk, and with directions in hand, made a beeline for the warehouse. Until someone tugged on her bag. He wrenched so hard it slipped off her shoulder. She caught the strap and yanked back, adding all her weight to the fight. The poor kid hadn't expected that and flew forward, his arm extended. He hit her in the face by accident then landed in a lump on the floor. Cursing a storm, the kind of words Dad had taught her, she held a palm to her throbbing eye, staggered then sat on the would-be-mugger. Fire shot through her skull and settled into an agonizing pulse while tears leaked from her offended eye socket.

With slow methodical movements, she unpeeled his grip on her bag, releasing her twitching eye to do so. "Listen here, kid. I wouldn't suggest mugging people in a mall. They have cameras, y'know, unless you're aching to get your ass caught. Fudgeknuckles, I thought criminals were smarter than this."

He wiggled, trying to crawl from under her, but she adjusted her weight, bounced on him a few times, and with a heel kick to his ribs, winded him. His struggles ceased.

A crowd gathered, and calls for security filled the quiet hum of the mall. She winced, not used to being the center of attention.

"Also, you made the silly assumption I need my bag. I don't." She bounced and winded him again when he tried to escape.

He glared at her, and his hoodie fell away, exposing tousled brown hair in need of a clean. He had beautiful eyes, and she could see this spinning off as a fat-woman-saves-rogue romance. If he wasn't…like seventeen or something.

Removing her thick notebook, she thumped him on the shoulder with it. "This, my dear boy, is my prized possession. I'd take a nipple clamp to keep it and inhale as many bottles of Adonis the government has in storage."

The poor man frowned, his expression implying she was a lunatic. Finding his torso surprisingly comfortable, she giggled. She wiggled her butt to the sound of his huffs and grunts.

"Miss, we'll take it from here." A security guard parted the crowd.

Tall, dark, and handsome, there wasn't a potbelly, and he was young and virile. Who could resist a man in uniform, especially when tattoos wrapped his bulging biceps? *Well, hello there.* She grimaced at the image of her mom saying that to the next Stan on her list.

"Oh." Jane shoved her book into her bag and looped the strap over her shoulder. She rocked forward, preparing to rise when the guard's hand appeared in her line of vision. Accepting it, she wondered why she was crying and her eye was on fire. Oh, now she remembered. Tousle-boy had socked her one.

A digital clock in a shop window showed she would miss her appointment with Max if she didn't hurry. No doubt the mall security would want to question her, then summon the police if she wanted to press charges. Sadness at not seeing Max filled her chest, mixed with relief, and the urge to burrow under her warm duvet. She took a moment to breathe, to convince herself this was what she wanted all along.

The guard crowded her, his fingers sliding from her hand to her elbow. She raised her face to his, her mouth parting on a question. His cologne, spicy mixed with masculinity, had her snatching a deep inhale, instead. Might as well milk this situation for all the feels.

"Um, Miss, your…ah…chest." The guard leaned over her as if to embrace her, and she lowered her gaze, slower than a snail's pace at what he implied.

Squeezing out of her dress was half her breast. Her cheeks, neck, chest, and good eye burst into flames, coating her skin in a fine layer of perspiration. Trying to act nonchalant, as if this happened often, *and* she had a degree in breast-juggling, she tucked it back in. She patted it as if to say, 'there you go, mama's got you.'

When he still crowded her, she checked her other breast, just in case. He stared or tried not to, looking like he had a twitch.

For lack of something to say, she forced a polite smile. "Thanks."

The crowd parted to the left of her, and Max strode through, his shoulders like the staff of Moses. Time slowed, and somehow inside a mall, a ray of sunlight fell across his golden hair. He pulled her away from the guard and cupped her face. Concern hardened his, and the fury he flicked at the kid, then the guard skittered shivers along her skin.

"Are you all right?" Like that, he had her attention, his rasping voice pebbling her nipples.

This day had gone to hell in a Bentley—escorted, protected, cherished like expensive cognac. Here she stood, center stage with her nipples hard.

Sucking in his delicious cologne, she grinned. "Sorry I'm late."

MAX EXPECTED HER NOT to show. He reminded himself over and over, as he paced in front of the sporting warehouse. Had he told her where to meet him? No, but she was a smart woman, she'd figure it out.

Time ticked, and he glowered at the warehouse staff every time they tried to shoo him. When security guards sprinted past him, he gave up on her coming. He'd stalk the park. She had to visit, at some point.

Jane. That's all he had on her. Not her full name and none of her contact details. His brain must have short-circuited. He failed to ask, guilty for accosting her and forcing his card on her. The decision to join any fitness or diet program required her full participation. He couldn't force her to change. Horse to the trough and all that.

Cursing at the crowd hindering his departure, he didn't expect to see Jane sitting on a young man's chest. Nor did he like the guard's proximity to her, and the pale softness of her semi-exposed breast tempting Max's gaze to linger. She tucked it away, jiggling her breasts. His throat squeezed, and his tongue dried. There was a reason why women didn't do that in public. His body shot darts of need to his groin as if he'd never seen a naked woman.

When she stepped into the guard's arms, lifting her bruised face, a haze of fury gripped Max, narrowing his focus. He tugged her out of the man's too-familiar embrace whose lust-filled gaze bellowed where his thoughts had gone.

Max asked her if she was all right, but she blinked at him with one unswollen eye.

He gave her a gentle shake. "Janey, sweetheart, are you okay?"

"Hey, sir, we need her details. The Rose Mall might press charges, but in case the police need her statement..." The muscled guard hovered, his bulk drawing Janey's attention; her cheeks burned bright pink to match her lipstick.

"Details? Sure." She rifled through her bag and handed him a card.

Max took the card stack from her, glanced at her name, then pocketed them. He slipped her bag from her shoulder and threw an arm around her, gathering her close. She feathered her fingers across his chest as if she didn't know where to touch. Just the fleeting warmth of her hand swept shivers through him.

She drew to halt, forcing him to do the same. "I didn't just tackle a man and expose myself to a bunch of people, did I, Max?"

He squeezed her arm. "You have a black eye too. Let's stop by a coffee shop."

"Coffee would be nice." Her distant voice alarmed him, and he tightened his arm, bringing her into the curve of his body.

He seated her then harassed the waiter for a glass of ice. While he stacked ice cubes in a cloth napkin, he fixed his gaze on the cappuccino the waitress placed on the table. A dot of cream rested on Janey's bottom lip.

He sat and offered her the makeshift ice pack. "I should take you to the hospital."

She licked her lips, and the air thickened between them. The pink of her tongue snagged his attention, and, just like that, he was hard. Fuck.

Holding the peas to her face, she scooped cream off the top of her cappuccino. "Cold compress, if bleeding or loss of vision then seek medical help." She sucked on her spoon, and he scowled, shifting in the chair to ease the growing ache.

"The guard was into you," he said.

"Not." She giggled, waving her spoon as if to dismiss the idea as nonsense. "He smelled good, but I prefer an Adonis."

Adonis? Max squeezed his eyes shut, a headache pinging in his temple. What did that even mean? She didn't have a concussion, right?

"We can postpone this." Not once had he considered he'd find himself in such a situation—about to shop with a concussed client.

"I took painkillers, so once I finish this coffee and you drag me through the sports shop with an ice pack on my face, I'm heading home." She raised her cup with reverence, leaving the ice on the table. "I've had enough excitement this week to last me a while."

While he downed his unsweetened iced tea, hoping to soothe his parched mouth, she savored her coffee.

She hesitated then blurted out, "Information mentioned an adult store on our way. I need to replenish my...toys, and find a better hiding spot for them."

What had she said? Toys? A shiver shot down his spine. He didn't want to imagine her orgasming, but curiosity won out. "What happened to your last toy?"

"My mother's trying out new things, but she wouldn't dare walk into such a shop or order it online." She cupped her head in her hands, the bag of peas forgotten. "No, steal and sterilize, that's her motto."

"Waiter." He raised his arm, needing to pay and get the hell out of there.

Amid sporting equipment, he was fine, safe. Whatever this was she roused in him, it burned with more intensity than an attack of lust. With her rebuffing his suggestions to postpone, he escorted her to the warehouse, steering her clear of the adult store. He needed an ice-cold, bone-chilling shower which could only happen as soon as he got home.

She grabbed five drawstring yoga pants, and super-sized T-shirts off the racks, two Fort-Knox sports bras, then browsed the sneaker aisle. All in under half an hour.

"If we're going to do this exercise *thing*," she shuddered, "I insist on paying for your time." She picked up a Nike all-rounder in her size, then tossed it in the basket, not checking the price. It was a good design, so he didn't argue.

"No, free of charge, as promised."

"Why, what do you get out of this?" She stomped her way around the customers to poke him in the chest. Her dress had plastered to her body, enhancing every curve, and he had thought it unflattering?

"The joy of..."

"No way, Max whatever-your-last-name-is, I'm not a charity case. You treat me like a client or I leave. Goodbye, cheerio, and thanks for the fish."

Whatever-your-last-name-is? He was a YouTube fitness guru, and he had worked hard for the title. And by client, did she mean one he wanted to fuck? What fish? "Max Reynolds. Half-price, take that or *you* can leave, Ms. Myerson." He folded his arms across his T-shirt-covered chest, and her gaze lowered, her brown eyes darkening.

She pressed the tip of her tongue to her bottom lip. "Agreed."

He nodded, looking anywhere but at her mouth. "Good, I want your full commitment." Using the guise of letting shoppers pass, he crowded her. "Janey, I need you to say it."

Guilt flickered across her face, and he wondered what she thought he wanted her to confess.

"Say you're committed to four months, no matter the weather." He brushed his thumb along her jaw, capturing a stray curl to tuck behind her ear.

"I'm committed...except—" She had nibbled most of her pink lipstick off. It drew his focus despite his best efforts, especially when she parted her mouth in mid-thought.

"No, no exceptions." He gripped the shelf to the right of her ear, pinning her in place. His mouth was inches from hers, and it would take no effort on his part to dip in for a taste.

"If my boss needs me, I have to obey." She gripped his hips and tugged him closer, peering around him to watch a shop assistant wheel a cart down the aisle. There were no other motives, no fluttering eyelashes, no pouting as if she wanted him to kiss her.

"Very well, work is the exception."

Her lips twitched, and a slow smile spread, dimpling her cheeks and warming her eyes. "If J.J. Cox needs me...us?"

He arched a brow. "How close are you to the author?"

"I've been her ARC for years. You'll need her details when you're done with book eight." Janey ducked under his arm, her hair tickling his skin. "I got you onto the list depending on your feedback. She doesn't need praise, just your thoughts, good or bad." She scooped up her basket, tossing a chuckle at him. "She loves a bit of sass."

So did he, and Janey had it in heaps.

"How much for four months of pain and suffering?" Planting the basket at her feet, she dragged her phone out of her bag he still held. "Give me a number, Max."

He rattled off an amount, half of what he usually charged for his time. A few clients neared the end of their sessions. His phone pinged asking for permission to synchronize with Jane Juliet Myerson. He accepted, and the amount popping up had him leveling a glare on her.

"It's too much, Janey."

"Say that again after a week of dealing with me." She picked up her basket, and slid it onto the counter, swiping for her purchases without acknowledging the amount. Was she independently wealthy, or did her job pay well?

With her bags in hand, he trailed her out of the warehouse. She paused, stepping to the side so shoppers wouldn't bother them. "I need you to say it, Max."

Ice drenched his chest. Say what? That she was turning out to be more of a distraction than his savior?

"Say you're committed to four months, no matter the weather." She raised her gaze to his, concern and fear darkening their chocolate depths. "I'm going to curse you, inflict epic levels of snark on you, and hate the sight of you."

He chuckled. "That's normal, sweetheart."

She gasped. "I need you to say it, Max."

With her bags weighing him down, he pressed his hand over his heart. "I commit to four months, no matter the weather."

She dipped her face as if she could hide the tears shimmering in her eyes. "Right, when and where do we start?" She wagged a finger at him. "You can take my chocolate," she winced, "and my cheese, but if you touch my coffee, I'll stab you with a spoon."

Max held up a palm. "Fine, coffee is untouchable."

"Maxy, darling, is that you?" A high-pitched sultry voice had him choking on a curse.

Chapter Four

Aphrodite would look like this woman, all long limbs, swaying lustrous hair, and pouting lips. Jane felt like a heifer at an auction, only good for breeding. *Step right up, share your seed with this sturdy woman, and she'll birth you many fine sons.*

Damn, she needed a photo of Aphrodite, tilting her hips and thrusting out her breasts. Fried eggs, her father would have said, not enough to satisfy a man. A glance at Max had her sighing. He glowered as if a bus had hit him, and the intrusion had pissed him off rather than floored him.

"Max, *sweetheart*, I can meet you at the jeweler?" Jane trailed a fingertip over a sculpted pec.

The woman's gasp was a horrified one, the burn of her condescension familiar to a plump woman. Jane was used to judgment based on her size. Max's reaction mattered more to her, and his lips twitched, humor warming his gray eyes.

"Yes, please, *love*. Give me a minute."

She shared a sweet smile with Ms. Gorgeous, and strolled down the walkway, stepping inside the adult toy store as if that was her intention all along.

Lesson number one; when in the company of a man as virile as Max, browsing an adult store has its hazards. Perspiration dribbled between her cleavage, and her breasts quivered under the constant abrasion of her dress. She waddled, squeezing her thighs tight enough to crack a walnut, hoping to minimize the throb between her legs.

Lesson number two; when choosing dildo sizes, bigger isn't usually better. One tipped up, promising to hit her G-spot without fail. The other had ridges. When the shop assistant confirmed the ridged-*and*-tipped one was out of stock, Jane had a dilemma.

Lesson number three; struggling with indecision requires external guidance, but don't ask the first person who walks in. Verify their qualifications before accepting their advice.

"Um, sorry, Ms. Myerson. I hoped you were still in the mall."

The handsome, sexy security guard flicked his focus between the packages in her hands. Trying not to feel embarrassed in yet another revealing incident, she held them up to cover her burning cheeks. She went with; if it doesn't bother him, it didn't bother her, and it wasn't her fault he had followed her into the adult store.

"Which one?" She fanned herself with the largest one, but at least her eye didn't throb anymore.

"It depends. The ridges should feel amazing, but the tipped would rush you over the edge." He took one from her and flipped it to read the back. "How long do the batteries last, and if you can afford it, why not buy both?"

Why hadn't she thought of it? "Good idea." She grinned and placed them onto the counter. "Here's a question for a man in security. Where can I hide them?"

"Hide?" He smirked, his brown eyes appraising her from her breasts to her hips and up to her lips.

She had been on the receiving end of many lascivious looks, as if plump girls would do anything, even a construction worker in a thong. This one didn't make her feel dirty or her skin crawl with a thousand judgmental ants. "Yes, from my mother."

His mouth parted on an 'oh,' and with that angular jaw of his, she could see the attraction. "Where most folks hide their drugs."

"She loves crime shows so that's a no-go." Under the bed, a broken floorboard, the air-conditioning vent, Jane had tried them all.

"Your car?"

She had thought of that too. "Nope, I'd have to traipse out it in the middle of the night."

"Why not buy a safe?" Max scowled from the doorway, his posture stiff.

She frowned, his anger unexpected. What? She couldn't talk to the guard? Or was he pissed she had deviated and browsed spectacular toys for her erotic enjoyment?

"I'll buy two safes so she doesn't abscond with my entire stash." Jane bounced on her toes, her new purchases dangling from her finger. Whatever bothered Max was on him. She had learned long ago that she couldn't change how people reacted. Their issues were their own.

Max strolled down the aisle toward her, uncaring that Sexy-Security blocked his path. "Are you done here?"

She jerked at the anger infusing Max's clipped tone. Was he a prude or did adult stores make him uncomfortable? The fury pouring from his heated gaze implied he was neither. It might have been Ms. Gorgeous who pissed him off, and his emotional turmoil had yet to dissolve.

"I'd like a quiet word with Ms. Myerson, sir. It's regarding the incident earlier." Mr. Uniform cupped her elbow and steered her into the changing booth, crowding her in.

"Need my statement?" She peered at him, conscious of his warm chest pressing against her sensitive breasts. Conscious? She snorted. What an understatement. Everything in her tingled, and she would have rushed home to test out her new purchases if Mom wasn't there.

"I need your yes to a date."

"Huh?" She gaped. Max had been right, but as surprises go, that one was a doozy. What was Mr. Uniform's intentions? "Why?"

"I can't say. It's many things or one thing. I'm compelled to see you again, and since you left with the runt," he flicked his thumb behind him, "I haven't stopped thinking about you."

Max, the runt? "How about a coffee, and we take it from there? After all, I don't even know your name." Eighty-two percent of her was screaming to run. She didn't do dates, but with Max eavesdropping, his sneakers peeking under the curtain, she wanted out of the booth as fast as possible.

"Carl Harris." He ran his finger along her padded collarbone, and down to her upper arm, squeezing her there. "I'm free Saturday, say ten at the Coffee Bistro?"

The curtains split open, and Max yanked her out. "She's busy."

"Max." She rested her hands on her hips, hoping he might get her out of this, but hating that he thought she couldn't date. "This is Carl, and we're going on a coffee date."

"When you don't know your schedule? You promised me four months, Janey." He tugged her out of the shop, leaving her to shrug at a gaping Carl.

"Will you slow down? I'm shorter, and as it is, I have to trot after you like a horny concubine."

He jerked to a halt and faced her. She slammed into his chest, her limbs splaying out mimicking a startled octopus. He looped an arm around her to steady her and glared into her eyes.

"We will focus on *you*, not your libido, nor your love life. Your health is a serious matter, Janey, not to be..." He exhaled, stepping away from her to run a hand over his face.

"Max, I'm sorry. I didn't expect Carl to ask me out, and I didn't think you'd mind if I kept myself busy during, y'know, Ms. Maxy-darling."

He slumped and nodded. "Morning or evening, which do you prefer?"

"Morning, then it's over and done with for the day, right?" For all she knew, he planned to torture her every waking moment.

"I'll pick you up at eight." He dumped her bags in her arms and strode off.

She would text him later with her address. The poor man, with his hand-tousled hair, dark brooding stare, and stiff walk, looked like he had suffered through one hell of a day.

Chapter Five

Max palmed his steering wheel, punching and slapping it until he felt more in control of his emotions. He hadn't slept well, tortured by Janey and her sexual antics. Worse, she had no idea how her words affected him. An experienced woman would hone in for the kill. Propositioning him hadn't occurred to Janey, as if she believed he would never find her attractive.

Such voluptuous role models were why Max loved J.J. Cox's novels. Her heroines were real women struggling with their self-esteem. He encountered that among all his clients, no matter their size or gender.

Six AM had him pounding the road for a jog, sprint, jog until sweat drenched his tank and exhaustion weakened his knees. He paused at the bottom of his driveway, leaned over, and gripped his knees, sucking in slow, deep breaths. He had time to shower, drop Abby off at school, and pick up his...client.

Which is where he was now, parked outside her house in a well-to-do neighborhood not far from his own. There had been no traffic since he knew the back roads. Squaring his shoulders, he texted he was outside. Her message last night with her address had added her number to his phone, so stealing her business cards wasn't needed.

With a resigned sigh, he climbed out of his navy-blue 1970 MG Midget and closed the door. He had been in a coupe kind of mood, but now he was rethinking it. Dad had left him the 1960 Chevrolet Impala, but since this was work and not a date, he should have brought the Audi. Max grimaced. Perhaps it was time to invest in something less...over the top?

She hurried up her uphill driveway—her eye swollen and purplish-black, waving him away. He frowned, narrowing his gaze.

"So help me, Max, if you don't hide that skinny ass of yours, I will tackle you to the ground." She nudged him into the bushes with a well-aimed hip and dived in after him. Curves engulfed him, her hands landing where they shouldn't, but she clambered up and clamped her hand over his mouth. With her citrus scent dazzling him and her breath feathering across his ear, she whispered, "My mom wants to meet you."

"Your mother?" Her hand muffled his words. When she nodded, he growled and tried to rise, but she plastered her body across his, pinning him to the ground.

"Look." She tugged him by the shoulder, her hand still across his mouth. Peering up the driveway was a petite woman in a revealing negligee and dainty slippers. Her coiffed hair and heavy make-up said she was ready for war.

He gaped. Wow, and she showed no signs of leaving.

"She hits on anything with a working appendage." Janey's voice softened further, as if she feared her mother would hear them from twenty yards.

He nipped at her palm, and she gasped, yanking her hand away. Pulling out his phone, he typed. "I have to meet her at some point, Janey." He didn't send the message, just showed it to her.

She slipped his phone out of his hands and typed back. "You're right, and I'm sorry. I panicked."

He dipped, forcing her to meet his gaze as he whispered, "You don't think I can handle her advances?"

She dropped her chin to her chest while chewing on her lip. For a moment, lost innocence and pain flitted across her eyes. With a pat on his bare thigh, she rose on her knees as if to reveal herself to her mom. He dropped his phone onto his lap, gripped her hips, and held her back.

"If you leave these bushes, you'll never live this down." He showed her his phone and waited before typing again. "Would she leave me alone if I pretend we're dating?"

She shrugged, but her stiff shoulders said he had struck something sensitive.

"Janey?" He whispered her name, and her bottom lip trembled.

She grabbed his phone and typed, her thumbs flying over the keys. "I don't know. I've never brought a date home."

Ice drenched Max's face, but he shook his head, trying to dispel the feeling. She used...toys, which meant she wasn't innocent.

"Ah, yes, your toys. Happy with your purchase?" As he typed it, his mind reeled, screaming at him not to ask. He persevered, needing her to cancel out last night's fantasies.

"I left them in the car. They're installing the safes this afternoon while Mom's at Zumba."

She hadn't used them yet, which meant tonight... He closed his eyes and inhaled, then exhaled, imagining ocean waves breaking onto the shore. Nice and easy, no lust, frustration, or jealousy here.

She jumped up, tugging him with surprising strength. "She's gone. Sorry, I can be a little impulsive."

While dusting off his gym shorts, she smacked parts of his ass, sending shards of pleasurable pain to his semi-hard cock. He lunged for his car, needing distance to thwart the temptation to kiss her. Bloody woman. He didn't open the passenger door for her, just vaulted in. Perhaps the morning session he had planned wasn't wise? It was too late, he couldn't cancel now.

She climbed in and tossed her bag onto the back seat. Her T-shirt and pants drowned her, and her sneakers glowed bright white. She buckled in then stroked the seat's camel-colored leather. He shivered, but faced forward, turning the key in the ignition.

"Love the car," she said, flashing a bright smile while running her fingers over everything.

"Building this was how I mourned my parents' deaths. I poured my heart and soul into it. The blue was an ode to Dad—his favorite color." Max steered the car onto the road, merging with traffic as he headed downtown.

"I adore antique cars, the older the better."

He smiled. "Do you go to car shows?"

"I used to before..." She looked away, silence dampening the space between them. "...Dad died."

Max remained quiet. He didn't utter meaningless condolences since he hated people doing that to him. Let him grieve and remember his parents without conforming to societal expectations.

A sweet smile teased the corner of her mouth. "What torture awaits me?"

He chuckled. "You'll see, and after yesterday, I think you'll love it."

A comfortable silence fell between them, and she raised her face to the morning sun. Pleasure, contentment, and peace filled her sigh. He tried not to snatch glances, to stare, because he felt the same way whenever he climbed into the MG.

He pulled into a parking spot outside the dojo, vaulting out of the car as soon as he switched the engine off. She opened and closed her door with a gentle touch, as if she respected the effort he had put into rebuilding it.

"I'll call her Bluebell." After stroking the bonnet, she adjusted her gym bag and waited for him at the base of the steps. She studied the facade and signage, her fingers twitching as she shuffled from foot to foot.

"Ready, Ms. Myerson?" He tried to smother a smile but failed.

She unclenched her jaw and drew in a deep breath. "Nope, Mr. Reynolds, but I committed."

"With payment upfront."

"Good point." She grinned and took the first step, then the next.

Relief slumped his shoulders. Horse to trough. He watched her climb, her ponytail and ass swaying, and he groaned, tossing a prayer skyward.

With a hand to the base of her spine, he ushered her through the reception area to the blue mats beyond. No feet pattered the floors, no legs thumped the boxing bags, and if it wasn't for the aroma of coffee, he would have thought Bryan had forgotten.

"Bry, we're here," he raised his gaze to the mezzanine.

The metal staircase shuddered as Bryan, all two-hundred pounds of him, clambered down from his office on the upper level. He strode toward Max, his hand outstretched for a shake even as he assessed Janey.

"The shake's for the lady, dumbass," Bryan said, snatching Janey's hand hanging by her side.

"Dumbass?" She twisted her lips, but her eyes warmed.

Bryan slid between them and, with a slight touch at her elbow, led her deeper into the dojo. He mouthed 'wow' to Max when Janey wasn't looking. "What brings you to my dojo?"

She chuckled, rocking on her toes. "Max mentioned something about my talent for sitting on people to shut them up. Do you teach classes in that? I was hoping to earn a black belt."

"Fully booked, I'm afraid." Bry paused and ran a delicate touch along her jaw. "Who did this?"

Her lips thinned as if she was in pain. "It was a mutual attempt. I yanked, he hadn't eaten for say five weeks, and like a perfect choreography, his fist collided with my face." She grinned through the pain. "He *was* scrawny for a mugger, right, Max?"

"According to my extensive knowledge of muggers and their migration patterns, I'd say yes." Where that had come from, Max couldn't say. Perhaps he had his own sass or being around her and her antics sparked it in him.

Surprised, Bry glanced at him, then laughter rumbled up his chest. "You must be good for the boy, Ms....?"

"Just Jane."

"Ah, Jane, Max has booked a slot for three times a week. I look forward to working with you."

"As much as I appreciate Max's enthusiasm, could someone please tell me what I'm in for? I mean, I don't mind a little Mixed Martial Arts or Krav Maga, but Muay Thai is O.U.T." The mat softened Janey's stomping, and she huffed. "Jiu-jitsu is a no for now until I can see my toes, and I lack the stamina for it, at present."

Max gaped.

Bry laughed again and draped his arm across her shoulders. "I think I'm in love."

"I'll be sure to steal Tanya from you then." Max had met Tanya first. That was a sore point for Bry. He hadn't meant to go for the jugular. Max's response had been instinctual, reminding Bry this was *his* Janey and a hint to her that Bry was married.

"Right, time's a-wasting." Bry rubbed his hands together with glee, a naughty twinkle in his brown eyes. "Shoes off and on the mat."

She darted over to Max, toed off her sneakers then showed him her back. She lifted her shirt, exposing her pale skin and blue sports bra. One clasp at the top remained undone. His fingers trembled as he hooked it before brushing his fingers down her back for a fleeting touch.

She stilled for a second. Her breath hitched, but she didn't glance at him.

They started with a warm-up, running back and forth, doing lunges, squats, and burpees. She grumbled, panted, and cursed with sweat plastering tendrils to her flushed cheeks.

He had feared this session, expecting Bry to use him as her sparring partner. That would happen at some point, but today, he didn't need to pin her to the ground or press his body to hers. His control was a little fragile.

The remaining time was spent learning stances with signs she'd done this before. The way she curled her fist, how she planted her weight, how she threw her body behind a punch or kick made him realize she'd left much out of her past experiences.

Max frowned. Needing a little more information than 'she had a work function,' he would have a word with her. He should've started with that or taken her for a protein smoothie. Any allergies for her eating plan? How sedentary was her lifestyle? What were her preferred exercises or sports? Did she have an aptitude for any?

The truth was, he tried not to think about her which wasn't helping his professionalism. He would have to focus if he wanted to bolster her confidence in time for the function.

She bowed to Bry then dropped on the stands beside Max to pull a towel out of her bag.

"I'd forgotten how satisfying and exhausting Krav Maga is." Her chest rose and fell with every labored breath, but she glowed with vitality.

Max glared at her, wishing the exercise had turned her into an unattractive mess. It hadn't, just a tomato-shaded version of her. "You couldn't tell me when we pulled into the parking lot?"

"What?" She paused in mid-pull from her water bottle. "It could've been yoga, although, I would've stolen Bluebell and left you here."

Right, so no yoga. "What else have you done?"

"Just Krav Maga for two years or so after Dad..." She shivered, jumped up, shoved her towel into the bag, and strode toward the door. "See you on Monday, Bry."

He waved from where he tidied the weights.

Max hurried to catch up to her, then paused when she draped her towel over the seat before climbing in. When would he realize he was out of his depth with her? "Time for a chat, Janey." He slid behind the wheel, buckled in, started the engine, and pulled out.

She closed her eyes and raised her face to the sunlight again.

"Let's start with the basics, any allergies?" he asked.

"None, and don't worry, I drafted a 'lifestyle' plan last night after stalking your YouTube channel. I brought it with me so you can review it."

He scowled, not liking that she did his job for him.

She opened her sparkling eyes, mischief in the twitch of her lips. "It was nice to see you in fewer clothes." The wind whipped away her laughter before he could fully appreciate it. "Ever considered running ahead like a Lindt on a stick? I'd follow you."

He clenched his jaw, sifting through the emotional rollercoaster invoked by her presence. She thought him handsome, but not in a romantic sense. Michelangelo's David might have sparked the same appreciation in her.

Max took turns to wipe his damp palms on his shorts, resignation squeezing his chest. There was an end-of-the-tunnel with Janey, and no matter what detour he took, he couldn't avoid it. Didn't want to, either.

He fought the attraction because he had committed four months to her. Perhaps afterward, when they no longer had promises and money between them, he'd ask her on a date. He clenched his jaw. Then she'd believe her toned self was what he liked, not the pre-four-months Janey. He ran a hand over his face, his thoughts hitting a solid wall.

Pulling into the drive-thru at Go Nuts, he ordered two peanut butter, roasted banana, dark chocolate smoothies. He handed her the containers and parked the MG in a vacant spot.

"I used to be active and tried everything at least once." Shrugging, she wrapped her lips around the straw and sucked hard. Once she tasted his favorite smoothie, her husky moan reverberated between them.

In desperation, he studied his container, running a thumb across the condensation. Waiting for her to continue, he drew in a slow, steady breath.

"Then my circumstances changed...family-wise, and it didn't matter anymore. I like anything outdoors, and if I can finish the session without noticing the time or the effort, bonus points." Her tight smile was self-mocking. "I sabotage any attempts to return to my former self."

Noted. "Are tennis and cycling okay with you?"

"I can't cycle, Max. My ass would swallow the seat." She kept a straight face for a second before giggling. "Your expression...priceless." She snorted then laughed again. Flicking away tears, she pressed the container to her temple as if it could cool her flushed face.

He may or may not have stared at her like she was a beef patty. She was going to kill him, but she didn't notice, sucking smoothie up her straw.

"I'll need to buy a bicycle, so whenever you have the time…" She rested her brown gaze on him, a sweet, sensual smile curling her lips.

He closed his eyes against the temptation. Not that it helped. In his mind, scenarios played out like a blooper reel. *Tossing the container out of the car as he yanked her into his arms? Cupping her backside as he dragged her onto his lap, not leaving the bushes for a solid hour?* How would the first kiss play out? Would he succumb, unable to endure another moment of torment? Would it be passionate, intense, consuming him in waves of lust and need? Would it be slow, tentative, the feathering of his lips across hers?

"Max, are you all right?" She touched his shoulder, her fingers burning him through the thin cotton. "Did you bump your head when I dragged you into the bushes?"

She opened the car door to place their containers on the paving before cupping his cheeks. "Sugar low, Maxy-darling?" She purred the endearment, then giggled when he glared at her.

He trapped her hands, drowning in her soft brown eyes. "I'm not partial to Maxy."

"Mm, same. Who was she?" Janey thrust out her bottom lip in an exaggerated pout. "Cheating on me already?"

"Look who's talking? Mr. Can't-keep-it-in-his-uniform?"

She laughed. "That's quite good."

Max smiled, unable to resist her humor. "She's an ex-client who thought paying for a personal trainer meant all the benefits."

Her mouth parted, exposing the pink of her tongue as she tutted. "The youth of today. I hope you didn't succumb to her seductive goddess wiles?"

Goddess? He frowned. Is that what Janey thought when she compared herself to women skinnier than her? As far as he was concerned, there was one goddess, and she was unaware of her 'wiles.' What if she knew she need only to crook her finger, and he would follow? He shuddered. Even Bry had seen and understood Max's interest.

If she could walk away from these four months seeing the goddess in her reflection no matter her size, it would be his greatest achievement.

Chapter Six

A FEW HOURS AFTER Max dropped her off, the stiffness set in. By nighttime, she was struggling to move. Mini-squats to pee burned her thighs, keeping Max's name on her lips. Dinner was tasteless so she skipped it, choosing to drown her hunger with unsweetened green tea.

Mom had a 'hot' date with Stan again which screamed purple pills. No way a man of his age had that much stamina. Jane gave him a month before Mom exhausted his pill-stash and bank balance.

They installed the safes that afternoon, but she had yet to use them. Her toys rested on her nightstand along with another print of book eight, Lone Rider. Hot compresses warmed her stiff muscles as she flipped through the channels, searching for inspiration or something to waste time.

Exhaustion drooped her eyes, but the day's events haunted her. Heat flushed her from breast to scalp whenever she remembered, and she buried her face in her pillow, trying to smother the shame. She had tackled the poor man into a bush. Fudgeknuckles, what must he think of her?

He had grunted when he had reviewed her eating plan, making minor corrections. His scowl said he hadn't liked her being proactive. Like she hadn't been on the diet rollercoaster before? Such a dumbass. Bry had been right about that.

Doing Krav Maga was invigorating, and she had the funds, so personal classes were a no-brainer. She could almost kiss Max for bringing it into her life again. Kiss Max? That toffee skin, those dimpled knees, and when she had sprawled across him, those hard edges.

Sweet honey on a bun, he was gorgeous. Every damn time she looked at him, he rattled her focus, her ability to function. She was hoping that in a week, her eyes would have adjusted. She tried to think of him as the older brother she never had. Or a dear friend who could see her at her worst and still tolerate her antics.

Now he wanted on her ARC list? Her nerves see-sawed like they did when she'd queried her first novel, *Lone Wolf*. Since then, she'd published nineteen novels. The standalones were as good, but not as loved as the Crossroad Biker series.

What would Max say if he knew J.J. Cox and Jane Juliet Myerson were one and the same? Would he hate her? Would he be furious with her for hiding it from him? Would she never see him again? No, he was a professional. If he couldn't forgive her, he would finish the four months *then* forget she existed.

Would he keep her close for her novels alone? Like that was all she brought to their friendship? It was the most she could hope for, and if she thought about it, friendship surpassed romantic dalliances. She would be in his life for longer.

With a moan, she adjusted the heat pads. She'd take it a day at a time and hope tomorrow wasn't as crazy. When Mom insisted on meeting him, she feared it would be a repeat of the Daniel-incident.

Her heart twanged like a too-tight elastic band eroded by family obligation. She switched off the television. She didn't need to think about him, how he had broken her heart. Mom assured her it was an accident, tripping on her nightgown, and flashing the poor man. Regardless, Daniel didn't return her calls after that. Not only did she lose the man she crushed on for over a year but her editor.

She spent days hunched over her laptop, dreaming of tattooed men with a strong sense of honor, visualizing knights on motorized horses rescuing hopeless damsels too fond of donuts. A taunt from Mom about her new hobby led to an immediate bout of querying. The rest was history.

She needed to think of another idea. As inspiring, panty-dropping sensual as the Crossroads Biker series was, she needed something new. She snorted. She should write about a lonely, dull-as-ditchwater spinster who wrote erotica in her spare time, falling for a hunk of some sort.

She chuckled, then moaned as her stomach muscles protested.

She would call the series...Spinsters at large? Boring Buxoms? Rubenesque Romantics? She grimaced. Fine, she would give it more thought.

Needing to write on her next novel, she peeled herself off her bed, heat pads tumbling like her hopes and dreams. Lowering herself into her swivel chair she moaned and straightened her legs. Within minutes she was elbows deep in Mr. Tom Bradshaw, a lawyer, and the grandson of Maude, who'd become addicted to erotica. He wanted to cancel her library card or hoped the librarian could restrict which books she read. Enter Amelia 'Amy' Perkins, a librarian by day, an erotic writer by night.

By four in the morning, Jane crawled into bed, seven-thousand words into her novel, and dreading seeing Max at eight. If he said anything about the dark circles under her eyes, she would blame Tousle-boy's punch. Possible scenarios between stubborn Tom and prim Amy delayed sleep further. If Jane wasn't due to sweat and drool over Max in the morning, she would have stayed up all night.

AT A QUARTER PAST eight, Max vaulted out of his MG to ring the bell on Jane's front gate. He'd booked a tennis court for nine and didn't want to be late. By the third lean on the buzzer, Mrs. Myerson's face appeared on the security screen.

"And you are?" She looked anywhere but at him.

"Good morning, ma'am. I'm Max, Janey's personal trainer. Will she be out shortly?"

The woman narrowed her eyes, then fluffed her hair. The gate clicked open as the screen flickered to black. With Janey's dire warnings ringing in his ears, he entered at his own peril.

Jogging down the driveway, Max admired the chaotic beauty of the garden, like an enchanted oasis with dancing Fae. He pursed his lips wondering if he had lost his mind. He had never thought of fairies before; didn't believe they existed.

The front door opened, and Mrs. Myerson waited, clothed from head to toe in flannel. Her slippers from yesterday were missing, and there was no make-up on her face. He couldn't find the resemblance between Janey and her mom. Hazel eyes with ash-blonde hair on a small frame, and plumpish lips. Not even the nose was the same.

"Good morning. She's upstairs." She gestured to the stairs curving up the side of the foyer. Beige walls, camel-colored marble flooring, and an elaborate wrought-iron balustrade drew his admiring gaze. Dark wood paneling hid doors leading off the room. Mrs. Myerson disappeared through one, and he caught a glimpse of a stone and steel kitchen.

He took the steps two at a time, calling Janey's name. On the landing, there was a double door that looked as if he stood outside an apartment. He tapped once and pushed the door open with two extended fingers.

"Janey?"

Her room was set up like a penthouse suite, as if she had reserved the top floor for her personal use. Wide sunlit spaces drenched the large bed to the right with an open bathroom. To the left were rows of shelves and hanging space, filled to the brim with her clothing, shoes, and accessories. Facing the large bay windows was a writing desk with a laptop on top. Books and J.J. Cox paraphernalia lined the walls around it.

Max strode to the right of the woman still in bed. She twitched as if she'd heard him enter.

"Mom, call 911, order a tall, blond Adonis, naked, and good with his thumbs." She had smashed her face into her pillow, a riot of curls obscuring her, muffling her words further. She wore a pink nightshirt, one leg thrown out of the blanket, bare from polka-dot painted toenails to her thigh. Heat pads littered the bed and floor, and on the nightstand were her unopened toys.

"Bring me orange juice, please. I need pain meds, stat." She moaned when she shifted her leg, exposing the sweet curve of her backside.

Max's breath caught, and he took a step before reining himself in. He frowned, having forgotten she'd suffer from her first day. He advised his clients to take it easy, not to overdo it, and to persevere through the weeks before their bodies adjusted. Janey had thrown all her energy into yesterday's session, but today's tennis would have eased the pain. He'd have to reschedule and take her on a walk, instead.

"Mom? Pain meds." She huffed, and flung out a hand, pointing at the bathroom.

Max smiled, fetched a glass of water, and shook two capsules onto her palm. She didn't move, just curled her fingers closed.

"I can't move. I think I've petrified." A sob escaped her, and pity welled within Max, constricting his chest. "If Max arrives, please make up an excuse. Tell him I died or ran away to Iceland." She sniffled. "I've always wanted to go there."

Max placed the glass behind her toys then scooped up the bottle of baby oil. He squirted a pool onto her thigh and rubbed. The smoothness and the heated silk of her skin under his thumbs had his eyes closing in blissful agony.

Janey jerked and tried to rise, but he pressed a palm to her lower back, insisting she stay down. She moaned and rolled onto her stomach.

"You don't have to do this, Mom. Andrea's son is available, right? He does make house calls, didn't you say?"

Andrea's son? Touching her like this with the same lustful thoughts? Not on Max's watch. It wasn't as if he hadn't done this for other clients. None of them were as sensual, delightful, enticing as Janey. His fingers trembled the higher he worked, but he closed his eyes again, choosing to avoid the temptation to lift her shirt for a peek.

Squirting oil on his palm, he worked the other leg. She peppered the silence with moans, sounds he hoped she'd make if he seduced her. Her legs glowed red by the time he finished. He fetched a towel from the bathroom to wipe the excess oil off then tossed it into the hamper.

"Better?"

Janey squealed, jerked up then slid off the bed, thumping onto the floor. Curls and a flushed face rose above the bed, and she gaped at him. Her nose glowed red as well, her eyes shimmering with tears.

"Max? What are you...? How did you...?"

"The fire station wouldn't release their man unless he remained fully clothed, and Andrea's son doesn't do house calls anymore." He grinned at her huffing and clambering to her feet amid a waterfall of curls. "I'd track you to Iceland."

Color burst from her cheeks to her heaving chest, flushing the sliver of skin the 'V' of her pink nightshirt revealed. She downed her pain meds, flashing him a glare over the rim of the glass.

"I'm going to kill my mother."

"What? No hello, Max, you look great in your tennis clothes? Or how about, oh, Max, I adore tennis, let me throw on something, and we can head for the court...*I booked*." He folded his arms across his chest, narrowing his eyes at her.

"You always look good in shorts. You don't need me to mention it. And yes, I do like tennis. I told you that yesterday." She stomped to her closet, yanking out gym clothes. "I worked late, like four-ish. So excuse me if I'm not as peppy as you expected."

"Four?" Max scowled. "You need eight hours every night without fail, Janey."

"Tell that to time zones." She opened closet doors, and they obscured her as she dressed. "I'm in agony too, starving, and I sense bitch-mode's on the horizon." She grumbled something he couldn't catch. "For the love of coffee…"

Humor twitched Max's lips, and he chuckled. She whined like a teenager. The end-of-the-resist-Janey-tunnel closed in, suffocating him yet excitement sparked along his skin setting him on this course of madness.

He squeezed his eyes shut against what he had to do. "A boot camp might be in order."

"A what?" She poked her head out for a moment then went back to complaining in hushed tones. "I hate these bras, like what the hell?" Huffs, grunts, curses, and thumps filled the room, along with exclamations of pain. "Torture devices created by the patriarchal society and adopted by women everywhere. Why can't my babies hang free?"

His mind envisioned them doing that, and he shuddered. "Men would prefer that, to be honest." He cleared his throat, wishing she didn't affect him this much. He adjusted his erection, secured by his tight briefs. A wise choice on his part.

"I wasn't talking to you, Max. Butt out." She closed the doors and stepped out in a replica of yesterday's outfit.

"Need me to do your last clip?" He was a masochistic fool to want to touch her any way he could. "Although, we're just walking this morning."

"Walking?" She dropped onto a chair to pull on socks, and sneakers.

"It helps when you have lactic acid build up in your muscles. Eight hours of sleep, and drinking fluids also eases the pain."

"Point made, smartass." She walked toward him, her arms raised as she pulled her hair into a ponytail.

"Insulting me this early, Janey? Me, innocent in my desire to see you well?" He pressed a hand to his chest, fluttering his eyelashes even as his heartbeat thumped a staccato rhythm.

"Next time I need to stay up late, I'll text you, and you can talk me down from the mountain." She met his gaze, stubbornness in the tilt of her chin.

"Works for me."

Janey climbed down the stairs, bending her legs with care. Pain twisted her features, and she whimpered with every step she took.

"Boot camp?" She arched a brow when they reached the bottom landing, pushing through a paneled door into the pristine kitchen. It had cream cupboards, a stone-topped island, the latest gadgets, and appliances. He would love to cook here for his YouTube channel, and perhaps, one day, she would let him.

"I need to check Abby's schedule, but I suggest, if you can take a vacation or work from anywhere, that we head for the cabin. There, I'll feed you according to the plan, and make sure you sleep."

She stilled, then lowered her gaze to the water filling her bottle. "For how long?"

"Five to fourteen days." It was only five, but with Janey, he wanted more time with her, to work on her stubbornness, of course. Nothing more. Fuck, he needed to make up his mind.

"Up, and leave civilization?" She drank from her bottle then capped it. "Do you have Wi-Fi, hot showers, and beds? Or will I be roughing it with twigs up my butt, and a nasty rash we're *hoping* is poison ivy?"

"Yes to the Wi-Fi, hot showers, and beds. No to the twigs and rash." Max chuckled wondering what antics she would get up to in the wild. If she shoved him onto a bed of pine needles, he might just keep her there. Tucking a stray curl behind her ear, he leaned in to whisper, "There is power too, Janey."

"Trevor's in South America for another three weeks, so I can work anywhere. Let me know when and where."

"You were an easy sell." The stone island would handle their weight. He could lift her onto it, spread her thighs, and swoop in for a kiss. He stepped back, not needing the warmth of her body to seep into his.

"I could do with a change of scenery." She chewed on her lip, as if she debated something. "Who's Abby?"

Chapter Seven

OH, SWEET MIRACLE OF Moses, Jane was pining for a taken man. How awkward would this boot camp be, two women lusting after Max? With her breasts squashed between chest and knee while tying a double-knot in her shoelace, what type of woman he liked was a face-palm moment. Her black eye twinged in anticipation like she would hit herself in the same spot.

How to make yourself more attractive by J.J. Cox.

Bruise both eyes. No man can resist such a woman. Be careful, face-palming can be dangerous. We want a light bruising, enough to generate sympathy.

She snorted then slumped her shoulders. Fudgeknuckles, this was an epic failure waiting to happen.

Although, with Mom out of the picture, there wouldn't be a Daniel-incident. Then again, the chances of Max finding out who she was had reached the stratosphere. Now she was backpedaling, trying to think of ways to extricate herself from make-out central. She would have to watch them cuddle in front of a roaring fire. Why hadn't she considered he wasn't single?

Because she was a romance author, and only single, emotionally-hurt-or-limited men applied for the position of the main male character. The female character was all levels of fudged-upness, but to be fair, Jane struggled to write anything normal. Boring people were boring to read. Give her bat-shit crazy, with a side-order of clumsiness, along with uber levels of snark, and she had the perfect femme fatale hocked up on sugar.

"She's my kid sister. I became her guardian when our parents died." His face softened.

There before her stood a man who adored his sister. Oh, that was all manner of wow. Jane's heart thumped. Bittersweet longing filled her with warm fuzzy hope chilled by raging despair.

If only a man thought about her like that, looked like that when he said her name. Mr. Right-for-her was somewhere on this planet, that she knew. Working an oil rig off Alaska and never leaving it? A research scientist drilling for ice samples in Antarctica? Orbiting the planet on the international space station? In a cabin on a hill in Iceland? No for the latter, she would have to learn their language.

"Ready?"

Jane nodded, shoved her phone in her pocket, and climbed the driveway, conscious of the hot-blooded male beside her. She pinched her lips, the stretching of her legs a pleasurable pain. Maybe she should come clean, admit she found him distracting, and ask if he could recommend a woman trainer.

Dad had raised a woman of her word. They had agreed on four months no matter the weather. She had paid him, and despite her inheritance filling her coffers, Jane didn't throw away money. Could she turn her back on him, considering how invested he was? It had felt like he had made a vow like he was a knight of the old order. Was his desire to see her well? She frowned. She *was* well. Did Max want her to lose forty pounds for his own reasons?

"Max, are you recording this for your channel?" She didn't like the idea; she hated it. She wasn't entertainment despite the novels she wrote. She, Jane Myerson, was a private woman, and hiding her true self was an uphill battle. Doing the book tour would announce to the world she was J.J. and open herself to ridicule or judgment.

"For my blog, but no images, and no names. Just how-to, and what not to do."

Oh, she could live with that. "You blog?"

"Every damn day." He chuckled.

Jane couldn't blog. Couldn't remember to do it, like a 'Dear Diary.' Wendy handled her website and other marketing stuff, leaving Jane to write. On a good day, she might remember to tweet something. By good, she meant an incident so embarrassing it was a choreographed tank-tastic failure. Those she had to share to warn others. Her do-good for the day.

"I've got to be more diligent." She had muttered it, but Max nodded, as if he agreed with her. Oh, to have someone to brainstorm with, to beta read chapters, to make sure she slept, ate, and soaked in a little sunlight.

"How long have you worked for Trevor?"

"Three years or so. Best job ever." Jane huffed.

She was shorter, and with Max's long strides, had to skip-jog to keep up with him. Was this his idea of a walk? She expected a lovely stroll, a slow stretching of her leg muscles, and a slight dewing of perspiration on her upper lip. At this pace, with sweat drenching her, and having tested out her whimpering voice for a horror movie, more pain awaited her tonight.

"I know you said my fireman couldn't make it. Maybe he's out on an emergency, and you want us to beat him there?"

"What?" Max paused.

She bent over, gripping her knees and sucking in air like a first-time free diver. This man was going to kill her. She studied his confused expression, wondering if he was an assassin?

She could imagine the newspaper headings.

THE SERIAL KILLER CONTINUES TO EVADE POLICE.

The Phantom strikes again, luring out his fourth plump victim. Ms. Myerson's body was discovered on the side of a quiet street, her new sneakers visible from deep within the bushes. The coroner announced the cause of death as heart failure.

"Sorry, Janey, I was lost in thought." He dropped into a few gentle lunges, encouraging her to mimic him.

She did. The pain in her thighs lessened, and her breathing evened out. Not her heart though, that had decided it preferred to do the rumba. His sculpted quadriceps were the kind you needed popcorn for. Watching the man lunge could be hours of wholesome entertainment if she looped the video.

"Is something bothering you? Want to talk about it?"

He jerked, surprised, as an unknown emotion crossed his face. "Thanks, I need to sort it out before I can talk about it." He tapped his temple and his chest above his heart.

"I'm here." She leaped up, bouncing on her toes, then swayed. Dizziness struck, spots circling her vision, her nose burning. She threw out a hand and gripped Max's forearm.

"Whoa." The dizziness persisted, and she sprawled on the sidewalk, uncaring about traffic, and the occasional sniffing dog.

"Janey?" Max's angelic face peered in her line of vision. Concern paled his toffee skin, and a pulse ticked at the base of his jaw.

"Just give me a minute, Gabriel, I'm not ready to leave." She closed her eyes, not needing the Adonis to send her heart into palpitations. Inhale, exhale, in, and out.

"This is twice in four days." Air brushed along her arm, and she peeked at him, now on his haunches beside her. "I'm calling a doctor."

"What? Why? So they can tell me I have anemia? Or that I should eat at regular intervals?" She snorted. "Had my check-up last month, Max. I am a healthy woman, my blood pressure is perfect for someone anemic. I have no cholesterol or the onset of diabetes. This belief of yours has to end. I'm overweight, not sick."

"You're anemic? Why didn't you say anything?"

"You asked about allergies. Except for a hatred for all things orange, I'm fine." She pushed up onto her elbows, the pavement digging into her skin.

Max bounded up and offered her his hand. She accepted it, and like the first time they met, found herself standing, as if she weighed nothing more than a feather.

"I don't think you're sick, Janey. You're just closed-off. I can't get information out of you unless I ask a specific question. As your personal trainer, I need to know you're anemic. I have to adjust your eating plan and not panic every time you drop to the ground." He cupped her cheeks, pinning her in place for his intense gray gaze. "How often does this happen? The dizziness or fainting spells?"

"Not often, only when I forget to eat."

He scowled. "Did you eat yesterday?"

Jane chewed on her lip, debating being truthful with him. His eyes had darkened, as if storm clouds gathered in their depths. He would kill her if he found out she could only remember the smoothie.

"Janey?"

She sighed. That rasping voice; like gravel rubbing along her arms. For some strange reason, she struggled to describe it, what it did to her senses. Nineteen books and she couldn't capture the exact sensation.

"I might have had lunch?"

He gripped her upper arms, his touch burning her skin through her T-shirt. "Please tell me you had dinner?"

She grinned, and his shoulders slumped as if relieved. "I definitely remember skipping dinner."

He shook her, his scowl back, and his jaw clenched. Releasing her, he caressed one hand down to her elbow, gripped her there, and spun on his heel to lead her home. She skip-jogged to keep up, huffing and panting, but he didn't slow down.

"Get in the car, Janey, or so help me..." He stared at her face for a long while, then removed his hand, his fingers twitching.

"What? You'll glare at me? I'm a grown woman, Max, I'm not scared of you."

He lunged for her, and she yelped, running around the car to climb in.

"You're a bully," she said into the silence.

"You're like a teenager, neglecting her body," he said as he slid into the driver's seat.

"Is not." Jane glared at him. "I have food, vitamins, body lotion, and toys."

Max groaned, thumping his steering wheel, and taking a corner too fast. "*Needs* as in *food*."

"I eat when I'm hungry, Max. I sleep when I'm tired, I orgasm when I'm horny. It looks like you want everything on a schedule. I don't do routine, but I've tried to form good habits." She stared at the passing scenery, tears burning behind her eyes. Dad had been a man of routine. He never slept in, rose at the same time every morning, and shaved every five days. She could set her calendar by his actions.

"I don't faint often because the sugar in my coffee kept me going, but I cut that out yesterday, sipped on iced green tea instead."

He remained silent, his knuckles white. Holy Moses, even his nostrils flared. She snuck glances at his ears, looking for steam. Nausea coiled in her stomach, and bile rose to choke her. She leaned back, closed her eyes, and drew in calm breaths.

"Max, pull over." Her voice was reed-thin. He didn't hear her or chose to ignore her. "Max!"

He swerved and jerked the car to a halt.

Janey flung open the door and threw up water and bile. He rubbed her back in long, slow strokes.

"Breathe. You overdid it, Janey. Most people stick to their eating plan in their first week, not skip their meals." The car lurched when he pulled the handbrake up, then he pressed his chest to her back as he hugged her. "I've got you, sweetheart."

There was nothing to throw up, a few more dry heaves, and she wiped her mouth, torn between sitting up or letting him hug her. It was nice, warm, comforting, and she couldn't remember when someone last hugged her. Come to think of it, he'd been quite affectionate in a caring sort of way. Like a brother or a friend.

"I'm okay," she said, and he moved off her, cool air replacing the warmth of his embrace. *Friend cared. Friend not like Janey hurt.* She harumphed at her caveman thoughts.

Just like that, she wanted more than his friendship. Oh, what a silly fool she was.

She buckled in again, and he started the car, pulling into traffic, but at a relaxed speed. Jane had stopped caring, preferring to lean back, raise her face to the sunlight, and focus on breathing. Maybe he had a right to worry? Her flushed, tingling face and the lingering taste of bile proved Max right.

She *was* being irresponsible.

Chapter Eight

SHE WAS GOING TO kill him. His emotions swerved from fuck-her to care-for-her, leaving his head spinning, and a pain gripping his chest. When she had dropped to the sidewalk, she was so pale, two bright pink spots on her cheeks in contrast.

Anemic? As if he didn't need to know. Skipped meals? He gripped the steering wheel, sliding glances at her. She had mentioned she tended to sabotage herself. This must be it. For someone so vivacious, so adorable, she hated herself, her life. He suspected it had to do with her dad's passing. She sought comfort in her work, losing herself in it to the detriment of her health. Perhaps she hadn't grieved? There wasn't a photo of her father in her room, nothing in the foyer; not that Max had seen all of her home.

On his driveway, he switched off the engine and peered at the steps to his front door. His house was a single-level ranch-style, squatting over the double garage. He might need to carry her up the steps.

His heart leaped. The thought of her filling his arms shouldn't have excited him, not under these circumstances. Would she let him carry her?

Janey opening the passenger door took the decision out of his hands. He vaulted out of the MG, hoping to stop her from attempting the climb on her own. She pressed her palm to his chest and met his gaze. Then she climbed one step at a time, her movements stiff, accompanied by groaning, her cheeks flushed. He hovered, raising his hands in case she tumbled.

"So help me, Max, if you don't stop, I'll wallop you." She paused, her breathing ragged, and punched him on his right pec.

"Hey!" He rubbed his stinging chest, her strength belying her weak state. "No fair, Janey. Threaten then punch? No time delay? What if I wanted to repent?"

She raised her brown eyes, exasperation in her arched brows and pinched lips. She nodded, rubbed then patted his pec. As if remote-controlled, his nipple puckered, not that she noticed.

"Sorry, Max." She gestured to the front door. "Want to get that?"

He darted around her and typed the code into the keypad. The door clicked, and he held it open for her. She stepped through and gasped, scanning his home from right to left. He tried to see it from her perspective. Large windows flooded light in from all angles, drenching his open plan lounge, and kitchen with warmth. White surfaces and gray fabrics added a crisp, modern feel.

"Oh, you have a fireplace!" She cut across his lounge, over his beige and gray rug, to run her fingertips across the course-slate mantel.

"Love fireplaces?" He chuckled and closed the door behind him.

The kitchen sprawled at the back of the room, and he headed there, planning to whip up breakfast for her. His chest swelled with delicious warmth, satisfying this need to care for her.

"Yes, so romantic." She slid onto a barstool at the island and watched him navigate the kitchen.

He pulled onions, peppers, thyme, and eggs out of his fridge. Pushing the carton of cherry tomatoes toward her, he set to mixing an omelet for her.

"I have these ingredients at home, y'know." She rested her elbow on the counter, and her chin on her palm.

"I didn't know, so coming here made more sense." He removed a bowl and broke two eggs then poured in three egg whites.

She hovered her hand over the carton then lowered it. "Um, do you have mouthwash?"

He nodded and gestured down the passage with a fork. "My room is at the end. Medicine cabinet."

Beating the egg mix with the fork, he watched her disappear into his room. He released a hushed groan, tempted to follow, to spin her onto his bed. What would she do if he let his desires take rein? Would she moan and writhe beneath him? Would she act the virgin, slapping him across the face for his audacity?

Everything within him challenged him to find out.

The aroma of heated coconut oil drew him from his fantasies. Feed the woman first before he exhausted her with his...ardor.

HIS HOME WAS BEAUTIFUL. Large windows framed manicured lawns and geometric hedges. At the back of his yard with a Japanese-style walkway, stood an enclosed pagoda. Serenity surrounded his bedroom, and his bed held prominence with panoramic views. The sheets and duvet were pristine. If Jane had a quarter, she would see if it bounced. The plump white pillows invited her to rest for a moment.

She gargled, studying her pale face in the mirror above the basin. Against her brown hair tugging out of her ponytail, she did look unwell. So much for spouting how healthy she was. She spat out the vile turquoise liquid, rinsed her mouth and the basin then replaced the bottle where she found it.

Drying her hands and face, she admired his bed again. Would his pillows smell like him? She hung up the towel, and peeked down the passage, listening to the sound of a knife on a chopping board. The aromas of onions, thyme, and eggs gurgled her stomach, but she swiveled on a heel.

She skirted the bed, standing at the nightstand with Lone Rider on it. Since she had to 'repair' the bed anyway, she threw herself across it and bounced once. She gulped down a giggle before snatching his pillow and burying her face into its fluffiness. She moaned, cuddling the pillow as if Max lay beside her. His scent drenched it and her nose. She drew in a deep breath, snuggling deeper into his bed, and sighed.

Lying down wasn't the best thing to do when exhaustion hounded her. She closed her eyes against the bright sunlight spilling across the wooden floor and bed, warming her feet through her sneakers.

Mother of Moses, she had almost fainted again. When last had she taken her iron supplements? She shook her head. She would start again today. Who knew what Max had planned for her? She couldn't faint every damn time she overdid things.

Her stomach wrenched, demanding she feed it.

Just a moment longer. She wanted to snuggle in his bed, as if she had the right to. Then she would hop up and straighten it. If this was one of her Crossroad Biker novels, she would expect the door to open, and a tall, muscled, tattooed Adonis to appear.

She giggled, willing herself not to roll over and watch the door. Max wasn't interested in her in that way, nor did she think he had a tattoo. Her heartbeat went through the three moves she could remember of the tango. Blue jelly babies, if he did have one, rippling as he moved, she would swallow her tongue. Would Tom Bradshaw have a tattoo, something harkening to his days at Harvard? What would Amy Perkins say about it? Or should Amy have a tattoo herself?

The bed dipped, and Jane registered it as far off, along with her sneakers falling off her feet. She moaned and buried herself deeper into the pillow, crushing it within her arms. "Oh, Tom, you're a sinner with those lips." Yes, good dialogue, but she doubted she'd remember it. Would Tom snatch demure Amy into his arms, or would he approach her with gentle sweeps of his lips?

"Who's Tom?" Max's voice penetrated her dreams, and she flicked a dismissive wrist, shooing him. Why did he have to appear in her thoughts? She was in the middle of creating an epic scene.

Where was she? Ah, yes, the first kiss between Tom and Amy.

Chapter Nine

WHO THE FUCK WAS Tom? No matter how many times he asked himself that, it spiked his heart rate. He didn't have an answer. He had no claim to Janey, had no right to cock-block her efforts to find someone meaningful.

Discovering her asleep on his bed and hugging his pillow touched something inside him he thought Emily had killed. He had sat on the bed and removed Janey's sneakers, then draped a blanket over her. He brushed curls off her face when he shouldn't have, and the desire to kiss her pressed on his control. He wanted her aware, willing, not dreaming of Prince Charming.

Tom? She'd never mentioned him.

He placed her omelet in the microwave and cleaned the kitchen, venting his frustrations and anger on scrubbing. One hour passed, two, and after he had recorded a video to upload later as well as undergone a kickboxing session in his studio, he was ready to face her.

First, to collect Abby from school. That took half an hour, his silence drawing concerned glances from his sister. Grabbing her school bag, he bounded up the stairs, expecting to find Janey in the lounge or the kitchen. The hum of appliances and bird songs from outside peppered the silence.

"My client is here." Max grimaced. How else could he explain his behavior?

"Where?" Abby draped her blazer over the chair and climbed onto the stool.

He poured her a glass of iced tea and started on a health sandwich for her. "On my bed."

Abby arched her brow then coughed on the sip of tea she had taken. "What? You've upgraded your services to full-body sessions in bed?"

He frowned, not liking his sister knowing anything about sex. "Ha-ha, so not funny. She worked until four this morning and crashed on my bed." He shrugged, but this was by no means a casual thing for him. As open yet introverted as Janey was, for her to fall asleep on his bed implied trust.

Then she called for Tom with his amazing lips.

Max scowled, hacking the lettuce with a little too much enthusiasm. Green bits splattered the chopping board, and he missed slicing his finger by a hair.

"Whoa, bad day?" Abby pinched random pieces of lettuce between her forefinger and thumb, and placed them on the chopping board.

"Frustrating." He closed his eyes for a moment, inhaled, and exhaled until he felt more in control of his emotions. "What's your schedule like? I need a boot camp."

"Hectic. Tests and exams, but I could stay at Dev's."

No, that was out of the question. As much as Max admired Devon's single mom for raising a daughter, he wouldn't foist his responsibilities on her. "I'll think of something else."

"Why can't she stay here? We have a spare bedroom, and you can do all your boot camp sessions in your studio."

He pursed his lips. Abby's suggestion meant having Janey in his home, all day and night. Not much different from the cabin, and with all the amenities too. The problem was she could leave and head home at any moment. In the woods, the closest neighbor was miles away.

"I'll talk to Janey. Having her here won't interfere with your studies?"

Abby bit into her cheese, lettuce, cucumber, tomato sandwich then shook her head, her mouth bulging.

"Hungry?" Max chuckled and refilled her glass. "How was school today? Sorry, I didn't ask in the car."

After a sip of tea, Abby grinned. "You did."

He sighed. "Sorry...again."

"What's got into you?" She leveled her gray eyes on him, so like his own.

"Max?" Janey's voice hitched his breath, and Abby laughed, as if he had somehow revealed his emotional turmoil.

"In here. Come meet my sister."

In a rumpled T-shirt, her sneakers dangling from her fingers, and her toes wiggling in her socks, stood Janey. Her brown hair cascaded down her back in disarray, one cheek glowed pink.

"I'm sorry I fell asleep. Your bed looked like something out of a Habitat magazine." She climbed onto the stool beside Abby and nudged his sister with her shoulder. "Nice to meet you, Abby. Your brother speaks highly of you."

"He should, I pay him in installments." Abby's expression remained serious, but Janey laughed.

"I should pay my mom. Favors, chocolate, what's the currency these days?"

Abby widened her smile. "Depends. What's your mom into?"

"You don't want to know." Janey picked up the fork Max placed beside her reheated omelet. "My mom is...eccentric." She frowned as if that was the only word she could think of to describe Mrs. Myerson. Selfish suited her better. Max wouldn't nominate her for the Mother of the Month award.

Janey's moan was deep and shiver-inducing as she forked the omelet into her mouth.

"I'm starving," she said, between mouthfuls, then threw out a finger to shush him. "Yes, Mr. Bossy Pants, I wouldn't be this hungry if I ate regular meals."

Max opened his mouth, planning on saying something funny. "Who's Tom?" He winced and whisked Abby's plate to the sink. "When you're done, I'll take you home." A glance at Abby found her giggling with a hand over her mouth.

"I'm off to do homework. It was great meeting you, *Janey*." She came around the island to place her glass in the sink. "Max and Janey sitting in a tree..." She whispered the words, but heat burst across his chest.

"Abby, please."

She paused, her gaze assessing his face before gaping. "You *do* care." She peered around Max to study Janey with her eyes closed as she savored each mouthful.

Max gripped the plate underwater with enough force to crack it. "Abby."

"I'm going." She threw up her hands, grabbed her blazer, and wheeled her school bag down the passage.

"Sorry again for sleeping. I know that's not part of the tone-Jane-to-with-in-an-inch-of-her-life plan." Janey sipped her iced tea, wrapping her lips along the rim of the glass.

"I spoke to Abby, and her schedule is full. Mind if we hold boot camp here?" He gestured to his home with a wide sweep of his arm, splattering dishwater on his clean, wooden floor.

"Works for me." She shrugged. "Anywhere not home is perfect."

"You have to promise not to leave the property. That's the beauty of the cabin, there's nowhere to escape to." He dried his hands on the kitchen towel before flicking it over his shoulder.

"Escape?" She narrowed her eyes, but her mouth twitched. "Is this a hostage situation? One where I pay you upfront to kidnap me?" Her gaze traveled the length of him, then, with a husky moan, she said, "Hello, Stockholm syndrome."

The air thickened with sexual tension spasming his balls. He gripped the counter, drawing in calming breaths. One look from Janey, that was it? He was made of sterner stuff. After all, Emily had used sex as a bartering tool, so he had the experience to deal with it.

Blue balls were like old buddies, and he knew how to handle those. There were certain pages in his J.J. Cox's novels he jerked off to. He needed to revisit those pages in the foreseeable future.

The bar stool scraped when Janey climbed off it. She dropped to her haunches to pull on her sneakers then rose to sweep her hair into a messy ponytail.

"I, Jane 'Plumpy' Myerson, promise not to leave the property." She grinned, tugging her phone out. "Mm, Carl phoned then texted. How soon can we start this boot camp?"

At the sound of the security guard's name, despair corroded his sanity, but hope was swift to strike. She wanted to avoid the man? "I thought you liked him?"

"I do, it's…" She bit her lip and gestured to her body. "We've only just started."

"He liked you without knowing you were embarking on a build-Janey's-confidence mission." Max scowled, wondering if he should help her hide or force her to face her insecurities? Who was he kidding? He didn't want her anywhere near Carl Harris.

Attempting to sound as if she was inconveniencing him, he sighed. "How about moving in tomorrow?"

"Perfect." Janey bounced on her toes, wobbling her breasts and swinging her ponytail.

"If you like, I can wait for you to pack, and you can come home with me this afternoon?" Max tried to keep the hope out of his voice. He needed to visit Bry and have him pummel some sense into him.

"That could work. Gym clothes, everyday wear, my laptop..." She grinned, ticking off items on her fingertips. "Deal."

"Excellent, and if we hurry, we can squeeze in Pilates before dinner."

Janey mouthed 'Pilates' and shuddered.

Max chuckled. "Relax, it's not like yoga."

"Whatever you say." She trailed him out to the car, and the urge to open the door gripped him.

Client, not girlfriend, he repeated *ad infinitum* until he was pulling out of his driveway with Janey strapped in the passenger seat.

"Please remind me to lock up my house. Mom has her cottage so if she wants to hold orgies in my absence, it won't be in my home."

Orgies? Don't look at her, focus. By sheer will, Max forced his gaze to remain on the cars ahead of him. "She would do that?"

Janey shrugged. "The way she's been acting since Dad died means anything is possible."

"Did she love your father?" He stopped at a traffic light, pulling up the handbrake. He kept his hand there, his fingers an inch from her thigh.

"In her way. I think he was her ticket to an easy life."

Max frowned, finding Janey's attitude strange for a daughter. "She's not your real mom?"

"If you mean biological, no. My mom died giving birth to me. Olivia is my step-mom from when I was four. She's the woman who raised me, but everything unraveled after Dad died." Her smile looked strained. "Now I'm her ticket to an easy life. I handle everything too mundane for her, although, Dad did leave her a sizable inheritance."

He parked at the top of her driveway and followed her inside. Sitting on her bed, he watched her pack her clothes, still on their hangers. When she tossed in her new toys, he snuck them out and hid them under the bed. She didn't notice, dropping her toiletries into a waterproof bag, before finding balls of socks and a towel or two.

It took longer to pack her desk. Her laptop and its paraphernalia went into a specialized travel bag. About a dozen notebooks disappeared into various pouches. She had a collection of pens that rivaled the stock at the local stationery store. Then in went the copy of Lone Rider which she snatched out of his hands.

Downstairs, she cleared out her fridge, putting any fresh produce in a bag, and left it on the front patio for her mom. She emptied the trash while he meandered through the rooms on the bottom floor. Her lounge had a massive fireplace, soft shaggy rug, and large brown leather couches he could sink into. Photographs of forests and lakes adorned the walls, and in the corner, close to the wraparound patio, was a piano. Irregular stone tiles in muted grays, browns added to the cabin-like feel of her home.

"Ready." Janey leaned against the door frame.

"You have no photos of your father." Max gestured to the black-framed sepia photos on her walls.

"Dad hated having his picture taken. I do have his piano and a few voice recordings from when he had left me messages." She folded her arms across her chest, hunching her shoulders.

"I hid my parents' photos for the first few years until I could look at their faces and remember the good times."

At the sight of her glossy eyes, he drew her into a hug, running his hand up and down her back. She burrowed into his embrace and unraveled her arms to slip around him. Contentment, like the warmth of sunlight on a winter's day, settled into his bones. He rubbed his chin across the crown of her head, wishing this moment could last a little longer.

She pulled away too soon. "Thanks." Her smile was tremulous. "I'll text Mom from the car."

Driving to his house, something heavy pressed on his emotions. It had a dirge-like feel, as if something within him had drawn to an end. Along with the sense of doom, was the excitement of new beginnings, the brightness of spring, the sweet sounds of birds. That joyful wonder added a bounce in his step as he unpacked the car and parked it in the garage. Janey lugged everything up the stairs and dumped it just past the door.

"Honey, I'm home." She laughed and wheeled her bag out of his way.

Abby appeared, a bright smile splitting her cheeks. "You're staying?" She bounced on her toes and punched the air. "I'll show you to your room. We have a Jack and Jill bathroom."

"Lead the way my sweet, fair, damsel." Smothered laughter crinkled Janey's eyes when she winked at him.

"Bring Janey to my study when you two are done." Max shook his head, doubting that they heard him. Minutes later, both doors closed, and muffled giggling followed. In a way, he appreciated how welcoming Abby was to Janey, and he loved how comfortable Janey was in his home.

Scooping up her laptop bag, he entered his study. Behind the door was his desk, set up with a massive screen mounted on the wall. He had installed mics, added lighting for effect, and padded walls for soundproofing. He could do Janey on his pristine desk, and Abby wouldn't hear.

Fuck, now that image would haunt him.

On the opposite side of his desk was an alcove facing the garden. It had served as his original work surface. Plug points were set into the white-stained wood, and the white-leather, swivel chair was comfortable enough for long hours of use. Her back would be to the door, but he had the windows tinted to control lighting and minimize the blinding sunlight.

Tucked in the corner behind her was a chaise lounge in gray leather with silver buttons. He never used it, but he could imagine Janey sprawled across it with a J.J. Cox book on her chest.

He didn't date curvaceous women when he had a reputation to protect and had just come out of a messy divorce. He might be on the rebound. Yet, as he slid her bag onto the surface, he couldn't shake the smile curling his lips. Whatever his thoughts and emotions were regarding his client, the following two weeks would be entertaining.

Chapter Ten

"WHAT YOU'RE ASKING ME to do is impossible." Jane huffed, unable to throw her hands in the air because she had to grip her knees to hold the position. She felt like a fudging pretzel. "I am fat, these rolls stop my knees from ever resting on my gentle bosom. You have balls, so how the hell are you managing it?"

She glared at him, then lowered her gaze, not willing to see every delicious muscle on display. He hadn't even earned a fine sheen of sweat while she, beside him, looked like a drowned rat. It didn't help that the full-length mirrors in his studio showed every muffin, donut, and hot dog she'd ever eaten.

Sprawled on her back doing hip thrusts added to about a million crunches. Work the core, he had said. If she wasn't sneaker-less, she would shove one down his throat. She had been elbows-deep in capturing the essence that was Tom Bradshaw, when on the dot, Max chased her to change.

Like clockwork. Routine and perfectionism. She had taken one look at his immaculate desk and known. Jane was all over the place, but there was an order in her chaos. She doubted he would see it that way. Two weeks of this?

She ignored the tears pressing behind her eyes. There was no escaping this or him. Besides, she wasn't being fair, having agreed to the boot camp. For the love of chocolate, she had let him into her life, and worse, her diet.

Four months to the unveiling. She tried to remind herself that she used to love exercising. When the pain burned and spasmed her muscles, such nostalgia fell to the wayside along with her convictions. She wanted to wallow in a tub of ice cream.

"Are we done?" She sucked in her pout so he wouldn't think she was a whining teenager.

"Almost. A few stretches, then yes."

He worked her through those, and she had to admit, they felt damn good, pulling on muscles she had locked into place when she hunched over her desk. Nothing felt as exhilarating as the cool breeze on her heated skin after the session was over. Like the epitome of freedom. In the recesses of her mind, a voice whispered of future torture, agony, suffering. That was tomorrow-Jane's problem.

"So, how was Pilates compared to yoga?" His bright smile irritated her, so she flicked him on the backside with her towel. He yelped and leaped out of the way.

"Okayish, doesn't mean I like it. The stretches at the end were the best." She opened the sliding door and stepped into the kitchen. "Want me to make dinner?"

"You can cook?" He smirked.

"Like my ass got this big nibbling on rabbit food?" She flashed him a sheepish smile. "No, I can't cook. I can wash dishes, that sort of thing. Need anything from the market, I'm your girl."

"Then why did you offer?"

"I assumed you have me on salads. Those I can make, and I haven't cut myself with a knife. Four days without an incident." She gave him a little of her jazz hands with a two-step.

He sighed as if the world was ending.

She had to resist the urge to check if the sky was falling.

Then he touched her face, dabbing at her trickling sweat with his towel. His touch was gentler than a feather on a baby's bottom, but he locked his gaze to hers. The gray of his eyes swirled and darkened before his focus shifted to her lips. His breath hitched, and his fingers trembled. He looped his towel around her neck and, grabbing both ends, tugged her closer.

Tingles exploded over her damp skin. The air thickened with sexual tension, the kind she captured in her novels. It must be her imagination, but she hoped not. A kiss from Max would fuel her dreams and fantasies.

"What's for dinner?" Abby's approaching voice broke the enchantment.

He closed his eyes, pain twisting his features before he met her gaze and unlooped his towel, setting Jane free.

"Roast chicken and salad." His voice was hoarse, sending shivers down her spine. "How about sweet potato fries?" He lingered on Jane's face for a moment longer.

She was an inch away from his broad back when he opened the fridge. Molten toffee muscles rippled as he moved, mesmerizing her. Her mouth dried, and she struggled to swallow. She panted as if she had run around the house.

"How was Pilates?" Abby climbed onto the barstool, a bright smile lighting her face.

Jane sidled past Max, not wanting to brush any part of her body against him. Between her mind, heart, and body, one of them was a traitor. "Um, fine." Embarrassment tingled her scalp. "I'm going to...um, shower."

She was a coward. What was she supposed to do? Her heart, and much lower, like past her belly button lower, believed he had been about to kiss her. Her mind laughed at the idea. Jane dashed to her bedroom, closing the door on a groan. What the fudgeknuckles had just happened? Pressing her palms and forehead to the door, she sucked in long breaths. Her giggles ruined any attempts to calm down.

She deepened her voice, squared her shoulders, and swaggered around the room. "Oh, Janey, I adore you. I've been in love with you since I licked mustard off your heaving bosom." Giggling again, she draped her towel and pajamas across the bed. "Right, idiot."

She stomped into the bathroom, closed the door to Abby's room, and turned on the shower. "You imagined it all. Stop living in your own world. Keep your head out of the clouds." She huffed. "Whatever, Mom."

Peeling off her sweaty clothes, she grimaced. She *had* imagined it. There was no way Adonis would go for dough-girl, all pasty white and...sticky. Her heart shattered anew, a sensation she was familiar with. Stepping under the hot spray, Jane sobbed, pain crushing her chest, gripping her ribs in a vise. Why would she expect anything else? Why did she set herself up for a broken heart every time she was brave enough to venture into the real world?

The lather from her shampoo mingled with her tears, washing away what little hope she had. It was time to accept she would be single forever and start naming her toys. A panic attack had her hyperventilating, tightness spreading up her neck and fusing her back muscles. It didn't help that her creative mind—the evil bastard—envisioned a wall of glass with a variety of toys, a collection of sorts. Each one would have a name engraved on a bronze plaque.

HERE LIES ROGER; HE HAD A GOOD INNING.

That's it. As soon as she returned from the book tour, she would sell her house, buy something in the woods, learn how to spit tobacco and shoot a shotgun.

A knock sliced through her downward spiral, and she hiccupped. She had left her bathroom door open, so if Max or Abby entered, they would see a whole lot of Jane's backside.

"Janey?"

For the love of Moses, anyone but him. She leaped out of the shower, skidding across the floor to tuck herself behind the bathroom door. "Yes?" She tried to sound casual, but her ragged breathing roughened her voice. Face-palming, she yelped, hitting her bruised eye.

The handle turned, and her bedroom door opened. Holy fudgeknuckles. Draped on her bed was her towel. She closed the bathroom door, leaving a sliver to see him through.

"I heard voices." Max studied her room. "Were you on a call?"

"No, no, just talking to myself." She swallowed past the lump in her throat, deciding it was the reason for her breathless voice. *Hi, you've reached oh-eight hundred, what pleasures do you seek?* She snorted at her silly thoughts.

"Then you made a noise as if you were in pain?" He stepped closer to the bathroom.

She tightened her grip on the handle, preparing to slam and bolt it. "I hit myself in the face." She forced a chuckle. "Mind passing my towel?"

He whisked her towel off the bed, then held it out to her.

She opened the door a little wider to take it, cool air caressing her neck, shoulder, and arm. "Thanks."

"Dinner's ready." He hesitated, ran his gaze along the gap as if he could see her naked body, then left, closing her bedroom door behind him.

She slumped, her feet skidding on the puddle of water beneath her. With frantic energy, she dried herself, rubbing her skin raw. If he came back, she wanted to be in her pajamas. No need to embarrass herself further by throwing herself at the poor man. Dressed in her fleece leggings and top, and with a towel around her head, she left her room.

The aroma of roast chicken greeted her, and she groaned, hurrying toward the kitchen. "I'm starving." She slid into a chair at the small round breakfast table. "A hippo was in the bathroom. I'll clean it up after dinner."

She raised her head when no one responded, having dipped it to inhale the steam floating up from the plate in front of her. "What?"

Abby giggled. "Your top's inside out." She popped a sweet potato fry into her mouth.

"I liked what you were wearing this morning." Max focused on cutting his chicken off the bone, but his cheeks had darkened.

Was he flirting? Her eye throbbed, and she let her breath out in a whoosh.

"Did you get soap in your eyes?" Abby bit into her chicken, then pointed with her fork. "They're red."

"Don't gesture with utensils, Abigail," Max snapped.

She rolled her eyes. "Yes, Maximillian."

Janey laughed, following Max's example, and sliced her chicken off the bone. "Yes to the soap and the utensils, even when one is beating eggs." She forked her chicken, a slice of tomato, lettuce, radish dipped in vinaigrette into her mouth and moaned. Soft, flavorful with hints of garlic, rosemary, and onion merging with the spicy radish, and sweet vinaigrette.

"Amazing, Max." She opened her eyes to grin at him. "Restaurant a le Maximillian or as Bry would say, a le Dumbass."

Abby giggled, and Max's shoulders relaxed a smidge.

"Want to watch a movie with me?" Abby gestured to the couch and the big screen TV mounted above the fireplace.

At the hope on her face, Jane's heart softened. Tom and Amy could wait a little longer, and the bathroom could air-dry. "Sure, but nothing sappy. Give me action, adventure, comedy, science fiction, or fantasy."

Abby gaped. "You don't like romantic movies?"

"Oh, hell, no. I can't be this happy if I watch sappy movies, and no to horror too."

"Thrillers?" Max dabbed at his mouth with his napkin. "Mixed genre like all the Aliens movies?"

Jane blinked, finding the exact curl of his mouth fascinating. One side of his bottom lip seemed fuller, and she wished she could test the feel of it. First with the pad of her thumb, then with the tip of her tongue. "Love..." She cleared her throat. "Aliens."

"I'm too young for it, Max says. Talk some sense into him, Janey." Abby batted her eyelashes and pouted.

Jane laughed, throwing out her palms as if to hide Abby's face. "No way. Max is right. Make a list of everything you want to watch when you turn sixteen, and we can hold a movie night."

He folded his napkin, dropped it onto the table, and rose. "Sounds like a good idea. We can convert the studio into a cinema."

Jane leaped to gather the dishes before he did. "With a projector and surround sound." She let water into the sink, preparing to wash.

"I'll do that," he said from behind her left shoulder. He placed a few items beside the plates then gripped her upper arms as if to move her.

She stilled, then shivered, reaching for the dishwashing liquid to hide how his touch affected her. It was insane to think she could feel his fingers through her thick top or her skin tingled where he touched her. Of course, she wrote such nonsense in her novels, but everyone knew that didn't happen in real life unless she developed an allergy to the person.

"I said I would do it, Max." She wriggled, hoping to dislodge his hands. Hers were wet, so she couldn't slap his away. "Help Abby choose a movie."

He squeezed her shoulders and released her. "Would you like coffee?"

Jane gasped, twisting to smile at him. "I would *love* one."

And they lived happily ever after. She snorted, scrubbing the plates and cutlery with too much force. Any man who offered coffee, the real deal and not the code word for sex, was a man to marry. "Did you wash the pots and pans?" No response. "Max?"

"Yes, I wash each item when I'm done with it." He offered her a drying cloth then held out her coffee.

"I don't like not contributing." She pouted, cradling the cup.

"You paid me, remember."

She huffed. "Half, Mr. Unreasonable. So meet me halfway on this too."

His tempting-as-sin lips twitched into a smile. "Fine."

"Was that so bad?" She couldn't resist teasing him.

"I'm making far too many concessions when it comes to you, Janey." He pressed his palm to her lower back to escort her to the lounge.

Darting forward, she hoped to minimize the effect of his touch. She lowered herself onto the couch, sinking into the right corner. Abby took the middle, Max on the left-hand side.

She managed Raiders of the Lost Ark, but halfway through the Temple of Doom, her eyelids drooped. Abby snuggled against her side, and with the added body warmth, Jane drifted off.

Chapter Eleven

Max chased Abby to bed, leaving him to deal with Janey. As soon as Abby left the couch, Janey rolled over, her head on the armrest with her back to the fireplace. He could leave her here, but the temperatures dipped around four in the morning, or he could carry her to his...*her* bed.

Wincing as he relived another eventful day, he doubted he would survive a week before he kissed her. Her smile, those big brown eyes, even her freckles were worthy of kisses. He had been so close to capturing her mouth, to claiming the woman tormenting him. So close to seeing her in the nude. He affected her too. She shivered when he touched her. Her pulse leaped when he almost kissed her, and when he handed her the bath towel, a flash of her breast was his reward.

With a gentle shake to awaken her, he called her name. She mumbled something.

"Janey?" He softened his voice, dropped to his haunches, and tried to slide his hand between her neck and the armrest. He would carry her to bed.

She rolled toward him, pressed her cheek against his bicep, laced her fingers through his hair, and kissed him.

At first, he froze. When he registered the softness of her lips and the sweet flicks of her tongue, he gathered her against him, sliding his hand from her hip to her waist to between her shoulder blades. Opening his mouth, he allowed her entry, not expecting the confident sweeps of her tongue, the soft sighs and gasps when she deepened the kiss.

His world, as he knew it, unraveled. She was hot, tart, with a wild flavor, and as addictive.

Groaning, he cupped the back of her head and kissed her like he dreamed of doing. Plundering the recesses of her mouth, he searched for that elusive essence that was Janey.

She broke the kiss, snuggled into his arm, and a satisfied smile curled her kiss-swollen lips. "Tom, your kisses are like sweet cherries."

Max jerked away, landing on his backside. At least his arm was free. He couldn't imagine her waking to find him trapped beneath her. She slept on, unaware of how she'd devastated him. Tom? He shuddered, jumping up to yell at her, but the words lodged in his throat. What could he say? No, it was better that he forget this happened. She didn't need to know they kissed.

He paced, wearing out the thread on his rug. Fury and desire fired along his veins, battling each other for supremacy. He shuddered, his limbs trembling. He lunged for her, then drew back to resume pacing. Rubbing his face and hair didn't help ease the tension pulsing through him.

"Max?" Janey stirred then stretched, arching her back. "What time is it?" She sat up and stared at him, her brow furrowed. "What's wrong?"

"What's wrong?" His roar startled her.

She clambered off the couch. "Shh, you'll wake Abby."

What the fuck? She's being the voice of reason? He stomped through the sliding door and slammed it shut behind him. He needed to burn off this anger, this frustration, and another round of kickboxing would help.

The sliding door opened, halting his rampage across the wooden walkway.

"Max, y'know you can speak to me about anything, right?"

She had no right to look worried, nibbling on her gorgeous lips as if she cared about him. He glared at her, needing to hurt her as the fiery burn of unrequited lust inflamed him. "Not about this, Ms. Myerson."

A flinch preceded the pain flitting across her face. She shrunk into herself, and the whisper of the door sliding was a death knell.

"Just fucking great. Why not add guilt? Why not add more pain? Twist a dagger into my heart, why don't you?" He yelled this at the moonlit sky, and now the neighbors' lights flickered on. "Fuck."

Sweat dripped off his chin, but he didn't stop. His knuckles burned red, but he punched harder. Every thought was met by a memory. There was nothing sweet about

Janey. She was a succubus, a sensual artisan, meddling with his emotions, bewitching his dreams.

Yet, as the energy and fury drained from him, logic returned. It was unfair to blame her. He hadn't revealed his intentions because he hadn't known them. He'd *decided* to wait, hadn't he? Why was this so confusing? Before, if he desired a woman, he would approach her, confident he would succeed. With Janey, she was more than a fuck.

His balls spasmed, as if he hadn't spent the better part of an hour trying to exhaust his body. Walking toward the house, the light in his study was on. Janey... He would need to apologize, perhaps explain. The memory of making her feel like a client, an outsider, when she was far from either, pinched his chest. She'd begun to blossom, so hurting her was inexcusable.

Max showered then pulled on a pair of yoga pants before heading to his study. She stilled, hearing him enter despite her headphones. She shook her head, as if denying he was there. Max closed the door, then rested his hand on her shoulder.

"I'm sorry, Janey."

She slumped, and her fingers hovered above her keyboard. She drew in a shuddering breath. "Do you want to talk about it?" Her voice was small as if she feared he'd blow up at her again.

"It won't make any difference, but thank you for the offer." He gripped her other shoulder, registering the tension in her muscles. As he worked the knots, she melted, moaning. He tried to ignore the sounds she made, accepting she was on this earth to torment him.

"I will visit a spa once a week. I didn't know I was this tense." She saved her document and dropped her hands onto her lap. With her hair in a loose braid, he had access to her neck and shoulders.

"What are you working on?" The title "Chapter Four" snagged his attention. "Are you writing a novel?"

She nodded. "A spinster series." Pain and pleasure strangled her voice.

"That's incredible, Janey. I didn't know you aspired to become an author."

She shrugged. "I thought I'd try. Y'know, follow in J.J. Cox's footsteps."

"What's it about?" Max broke away and sat on the edge of the chaise lounge, clasping his hands between his knees. One tug and she would be naked to the waist. One kiss and she would know how much he wanted her. His nostrils flared, but he forced a smile, hoping to encourage her to share. It would go a long way to ease the tension in the air.

"She's a librarian by day and an erotic writer by night. He's a tight-assed lawyer trying to stop his grandmother from reading smut." A dreamy smile curled her mouth and softened her eyes. "I have two options for their first kiss."

"What do you have planned?"

She swiveled the chair, her face brightening. Her eyes were red-rimmed, indicative of her crying, but she glowed with excitement. "Want to brainstorm with me?"

Her gaze lingered on his bare chest, lowering to the waistband of his pants before looking away. Fresh color flushed her cheeks, with the blush traveling lower to disappear into her top. He liked watching her admire his body, liked how much he unnerved her.

"Sure." Her enthusiasm was addictive, and if it was a way to convey his sincerest regret, he would listen to her drone on about her novel.

"Right, I have the dialogue, sort of. She says he has sinner's lips, or they're as sweet as cherries. I can't decide. I thought I'd write it, and see how it reads."

Max stilled, ice drenching his face. He cleared his throat, his breathing ragged. "I need their names; I can't call them Him and Her."

"Oh." Janey bounced in her chair. "Amelia Perkins and Tom Bradshaw."

"Tom?" He groaned, dropping his face into his hands. Laughter rumbled in his belly then bubbled up. He, Maximillian Reynolds, was an idiot.

"Is Tom a bad name?" Janey's frown started another round of laughter.

"It's...perfect." Max managed to speak between chuckles. Tears streamed from his eyes which he rubbed away, happier at that moment than he could remember.

"She's ignoring him again, packing books onto the returns trolley when he grabs and kisses her." Janey frowned. "Too cliché?"

Max struggled to answer. Fuck, he wished he could grab and kiss Janey. Now that he knew Tom wasn't real, he would pursue her with every breath in his body. "I don't know. I'm struggling to envision it." He rose, tugged her hand into his, and pulled her out of her chair.

"Let's pretend this is the trolley." He pushed the chair between them.

"Role-playing?" She worried her bottom lip. "I've never done this before."

"Let's try it." Delicious anticipation curled in his chest and settled in his groin. "Pretend to pack books and ignore me."

To his amazement and delight, she did, stacking invisible books. He struggled to hide his smile and the lust pooling in him from his toes to his taut nipples.

"Ms. Perkins, I insist you help me with this. My grandmother should not be reading this filth." Max gestured to the 'library' with a twirling forefinger.

"There is no law against these books, Mr. Bradshaw. You of all people should know that." Janey pushed up her imaginary eyeglasses then ruined it with, "I'm loving this. We should record this, Max."

"Focus, Janey." Max settled a fake-glower on her. "I know the law, Ms. Perkins, but as her grandson, I care about her wellbeing."

"Um...Smut does no harm. Many scientific journals publish results on how beneficial sexual release is to one's health. You'll find those in the 500 section."

"You want healthy, eat a fucking apple, Ms. Perkins."

"Language." Janey huffed then giggled. "Then he kisses her?"

"He grabs her like this." Max wrapped his fingers around her upper arms and yanked her to him with the chair between them. "What type of kiss is it, Janey? Soft?"

She blinked at him, her smile fading, and her eyes darkening. She kept her body stiff, as if she didn't believe he would kiss her.

He lowered his head at a snail's pace, drowning in her chocolate eyes, and giving her time to pull away. When she didn't, elation energized him, and the urge to devour her tore through him. He gathered his control and brushed his mouth across hers, testing the softness of each lip, planting tiny kisses at the corners, tugging on the bottom lip with his teeth. She moaned, and the tremble that rippled through her flowed up his arms.

She gasped, then lunged back. The gentle slap across his cheek took him by surprise. Amelia might do that, but Janey wouldn't slap him for kissing her. Tom might storm off, but Max wouldn't walk away.

Grabbing her arms again, he dragged her around the chair and kissed her hard. He fused his lips to hers, as if he couldn't get enough of her taste, the perfume of her skin, the way she moaned beneath his onslaught. Her fingertips dug into his abs, burning him, urging him on.

Releasing her upper arms, he glided his hands across her back to pull her closer, her softness engulfing him. He gentled the kiss, then broke away to spread tiny kisses along her jaw.

"Is this what you mean by brainstorming?" He smothered a chuckle at her dazed yet heated expression.

She nodded, pressing four fingers to her swollen lips.

He planned many of these incidences, wanting her to suffer, to yearn as he did. Tit for tat, so to speak. He hadn't lasted four days. How long would inexperienced Janey last? Then, when every inch of her ached for him, he'd cease this game, this torment, and fuck her. Hard, gentle, wild, he didn't care.

He ushered her to bed, then grabbed a J.J. Cox off the shelf. Time to make use of certain earmarked pages. Although, with Janey in the house, he doubted he needed help.

Chapter Twelve

JANE CRADLED HER COFFEE, reeling from Max's kisses. Half of her enjoyed the wild emotions churning inside her, the zing of excitement, and the escaping sighs. The other half had fear ricocheting in her mind. He was messing with her. It hadn't happened, and if it had, they were role-playing.

Then Mr. Stud Muffin stepped into the kitchen in jeans and a white, button-up shirt looking more delicious than an all-you-can-eat dessert buffet. His hair, damp from a shower, fell across his temple. He had left a few buttons undone, revealing soft-looking, pale-gold hair on his chest. His cologne filled the air, and she paused mid-sip to inhale pure, unadulterated masculinity.

Max kissed Abby on the temple.

Jane scanned the room looking for hidden cameras because this sure as hell looked like an advertisement for men's soap, a cologne, or GQ magazine. The brush of his lips across her ear, the feather of his fingers along her nape sent shivers along her skin. Heat spread from her breasts to her core, like a bolt of lightning, and she squirmed on the barstool.

Her lady bits throbbed, and she couldn't find her toys. She was pretty sure she had packed them. A snapshot of them lying in her bag came to mind, yet they weren't with her. Which left her fingers, and for what she was feeling, they weren't adequate.

She had to fight whatever this was. He had to see her as an easy target, a challenge, or a bet because there was no way, on this side of the equator, that a man like him could find her attractive.

"Morning." Jane hid her face in her cup.

Don't look at his long legs molded in denim.

Don't stare at that tight backside, and do not linger on the smooth toffee of his skin.

No, you cannot lick him. It's against the law everywhere to lick people.

Dammit, he smelled so good.

"Someone's in a good mood." Abby spooned cereal into her mouth.

"Was thinking of bacon, eggs, mushrooms, or..." Max grinned. "Pancakes?"

"What the hell?" Abby dropped her spoon into the bowl, splashing milk onto the counter.

"Language." Max took Janey's cup out of her hands and poured the contents down the drain.

She moaned, throwing out a hand to stop him. Mother of Moses, she could enjoy only two cups a day. She glared at him, and he skirted the counter to frame her face holding her still for a sweet kiss that set her lips on fire. How did he do that? Of course, her never-silent, always-demanding lady bits wanted her to sink into the kiss.

"Whoa." Abby paused in her milk-clean-up operation. "What's this?"

"It's me trying to convince Janey to have breakfast with me."

Abby rolled her eyes. "Go, Janey, before he turns into Tight-ass Max again."

"Language," Max said, but he didn't break eye contact, his gray gaze boring into Jane's.

"I can't eat pancakes." What? That was all her befuddled mind could come up with. *Smooth, Ms. Cosmopolitan.*

"You can on cheat day."

She froze. That's today? She cupped his hands, holding him in place. "I can eat anything I want?"

He licked his lips as if he savored her flavor. "If you return to the eating plan tomorrow."

Right now, as delicious as Max was, she dreamed of black-pepper-crusted steak with blue-cheese drenching it. "Then yes, but on one condition."

He lingered on her lips as he stroked his thumb along her bottom one. "Name it." With her back to Abby, she couldn't see how her brother tormented Jane.

She tried to hold onto her thoughts when his touch disrupted the connection between her brain and tongue. "I treat you both to dinner at my favorite restaurant."

"I'm in." Abby darted around them to hug Max from behind, jumping up and down and dislodging his hands on Jane's face. "Say yes, please, Max."

"If you quit hugging me, then we can go." He spun and caught his sister, tossing her into the air. She squealed then thumped him on the arm.

"Let me put on a bra." Jane closed her eyes. She hadn't just said that. Oh, blue jelly babies, please let him not have heard her. She darted into her room and closed the door.

She tugged on a pair of jeans, matching his dress code, and a pale-blue, off-the-shoulder baggy shirt that clung to her when she moved. The brush of fabric made her feel sexy, and the clinginess of the fabric canceled the baggy factor. She had bought a few of these in as many colors as she could find.

She slipped into dark-blue peep-toe wedges, then admired her choices in the bathroom mirror. With a brush of her hair, a little make-up, concealer, and mauve lipstick, she was ready. Oh, perfume. She didn't often wear it, but this was a special occasion. One should always dress for bacon.

Sniffing the bottle, she smiled. Citrus, grass, cinnamon, and maybe vanilla? Applying it, she pulled the shirt over her backside, draping it better, then slipped her phone and bank card into her back pocket.

"I'm ready," she said, swaggering into the kitchen to kiss Abby on the temple. "I was thinking of bacon, eggs..." Jane ruined her Max-impersonation with a chuckle. "Need anything, Abby-babe?"

"Mm, in the immortal words of J.J. Cox, a semi-naked fireman with an appetite for..."

"Abby!" Max's face paled, and he gripped his sister by the shoulders. "Please, please, tell me you haven't been reading—"

"Only the underlined parts." She shrugged, but she blushed. "I figured they had to mean something if you like them so much."

Max growled, stomped to the bookshelf, scooped off his J.J. Cox collection, then disappeared down the passage.

Abby watched until his door closed. "Now that he's gone, ice cream, please, Janey, or chocolate."

Jane gaped. "How... You didn't..."

Abby rolled her eyes and huffed a lock of hair out of her face. "I know about sex. We have sex-ed class, and the kids at school talk. Max wants to keep me a five-year-old forever."

"It's his right as your brother and guardian. It would kill him to lose you or see you unhappy."

She sighed, her little chin resting on her chest. "I know."

Jane offered a smile. "Any particular chocolate?"

She swallowed her tongue, not hearing Abby's reply.

Striding down the passage, his hair fell away from his face, his thigh muscles rippled, and she had an image of herself lying beneath him. She went hot then cold, her body shivering in anticipation. Oh, and she had stopped breathing.

When that happened, the body took over, and her loud sucking in of air, as necessary as it was for life, had her rushing to the door with her head lowered. She waved to Abby and hurried down the steps to the garage.

Jane raised her face to the morning sunlight, basking in its warmth as she waited for Max. A gentle breeze teased her hair and cooled her cheeks. There was nowhere else she wanted to be.

"You look breathtaking." Max's shadow fell across her.

She opened her eyes. "Um...thanks."

He crowded her, and she stepped back, but he matched her step. Confused, she frowned, meeting his determined expression with an arched brow. He caressed her chin, her jaw, and buried his fingers in her hair behind her ears, tilting her face.

"I mean it, Janey. You in those jeans..." He paused, his nostrils flared, and a guttural groan tore from him. "Fuck, you smell good."

Using his hips, he pushed her back until she bumped into the garage door, then pinned her there. He braced his weight on his hands on either side of her head. She raised her palms to his chest, not sure if she wanted to push him away—oh, fudgeknuckles, no—or dig her fingers into his shirt, and yank him closer. The heat of his skin pouring through the thin cotton shirt had her digging her fingers in any way.

He groaned and shifted, his hard edges layering, trapping her. Dipping his head, he buried his face into the curve of her neck, grumbling something she couldn't decipher. Before she could ask him to repeat it, he kissed her exposed collarbone and ran his lips along the column of her neck.

Lust slammed hard, uncaring, unforgiving, and she shuddered under the onslaught. Everything tingled, from scalp to skin, from nipples to toes, as an intense hot need pooled at the juncture of her thighs.

"I'm not Amelia." Her voice was the feminine version of gravel meets tarmac.

He jerked back. His gray gaze settled on her face and lingered there. Intensity hardened his jaw and darkened his cheeks. "I kissed Janey, not Amelia."

Lacing his fingers through hers, he tugged her away from the garage door as it opened.

She gaped, having expected a double garage, but this was two-cars deep, holding the MG, with a silver Audi next to it. To the rear were a Chevrolet Impala, and a matte-black motorcycle.

"You ride motorcycles?" She scanned his body, searching for a shadow of a tattoo.

"Lone Wolf had me rushing out to buy one."

Joy, like nothing she had felt before, consumed her. The elation, the heat, the fuzzy feeling that rose from her belly to her chest to her heart had her ducking her head to hide the tears. She had never thought her stories could impact someone's life like this. When she stepped onto that plane in four months, she would remember this moment.

She climbed into the MG, not wanting him to feel he had to open the door for her. The sexual tension between them sizzled, and the memory of his kisses curled her toes; still, she shouldn't make assumptions about their relationship.

Fudging blue jelly babies, if she fell for him—which was a growing possibility—it would break her heart when she could no longer see him. Friendship, remember, that was all she could ask for. A casual affair would mean losing him forever.

Her heart beat a mile a minute and tried to escape up her throat. She snuck a glance at him as he pulled onto the road, his long-fingered hands gripping the steering wheel with confidence. Her scrambling was too late.

She was in love with Maximillian Reynolds and so screwed.

Chapter Thirteen

Max didn't believe in cheat days, yet here he was, at breakfast with the woman who haunted his dreams. When he'd settled into the booth, the waiter had brought him a glass of ice, no doubt remembering the last time he and Janey had a coffee here.

One eye-twinkle from her, and his heart skipped a beat. He'd stalled in the shower, needing Abby to start on cereal while hoping Janey stayed true to herself and only made coffee.

Fuck.

Janey in a dress with *no bra*, in jeans that hugged her curves, in a shirt baring her shoulder, and in that perfume. He groaned, closing his eyes as if he enjoyed the tasteless omelet on his plate. He'd like her with nothing on but the perfume and those shoes.

She'd followed his example and chosen a Spanish omelet but pushed it around her plate. The cream had congealed on her cappuccino, and she sighed, her shoulders slumping, as if something awful had happened.

The woman who had emerged from her bedroom looking like a sex goddess now acted like an emo teenager.

"What's wrong?"

"I'm sad I'm not enjoying this. It tastes…oily." She smiled, but it didn't reach her eyes. "I prefer your cooking, to be honest."

"I'll make you breakfast next Saturday."

Her breath hitched, and sadness trembled her cheeks as she struggled to contain her emotions. She dipped her face, trying to hide from him. *What the hell?*

"I meant this as a treat, Janey. Sweetheart, you're scaring me." He put his fork down to reach across the table.

She jerked, then leaped to her feet, tossing her napkin on the table. "I'll use the ladies' room, and meet you by Bluebell."

Max gaped after her, watching until he could no longer see her. Something cold, hard, and burning skewered his heart. Had he said something he shouldn't have? Done anything to upset her? Come to think of it, she had been quiet on the drive over.

He paid for the disappointing meal and meandered to the mall's parking lot. Were his advances too intense? Was she an inexperienced woman unable to say no? He shook his head. She kissed him back, scraped her nails across his scalp, shoulders, and any part of him she could reach. He rested his backside on the front fender, crossed his legs at the ankles, and waited.

The sway of her hair, hips, and breasts snagged his attention, and he stared, unable to resist absorbing her sensuality. He had thought her drab, a spinster in need of saving as much as he needed a lifeline. The fire, electricity, adrenaline burning his veins, his senses, along his skin, had nothing to do with rescuing.

Was he on the rebound? Hell, no.

She stopped and spun on her heel as Carl Harris jogged toward her.

Max gritted his teeth and pushed off his car. He didn't focus on Carl though, he needed her reactions to reveal how she felt about the muscled gorilla. Her hands remained at her side, one swinging a labeled shopping bag he recognized. Had she really used the ladies or had that been an excuse to buy chocolates?

Max watched their body language, wishing he could read lips.

She pointed at him, her shoulders sagging for a moment before she squared them. She shook her head, gripped Carl's forearm, then walked away, not once looking back. Max spared a glance at the security guard, catching the lust-drenched sadness on his face.

Had Janey rejected the man?

Max released a long breath, tingles settling in his knees and bubbling to his groin. Was Carl out of the picture? Joy filled every inch and pore of his body, and he wanted to whoop, to dance, to fist-pump. Instead, he ran another admiring gaze over her. She slowed her approach, the bag no longer swinging.

Gone was her enthusiasm, and she climbed into his car without a word. "If you don't mind, I bought Abby a little chocolate. Teenage girls need it, especially on certain days of the month."

Didn't he know that? Abby's harassment while he was showering, her need for chocolate ice cream?

"Noted. I'll stock up for those emergencies." He didn't start the engine but twisted in his seat to face her. "What's wrong, Janey? The truth now."

"I..." She bit her lip, tears shimmering on her eyelashes.

The sight of them had him reaching across the handbrake to hug her.

"I'm...sorry." She rubbed her face across his shoulder, along his collarbone. "I need some alone time. I'm not used to company."

She wanted to hide from the world, to withdraw, either from him or the emotions he invoked in her. He could grant her this, but not fully. He would give her the space she needed, but he would be on the outskirts, Abby too.

"Quiet time until dinner?" He brushed away the tears. Fuck, even like this, he wanted her. Couldn't she see that?

"That would be wonderful." She pulled away, buckled in, and curled into herself, as far from him as she could in the small confines of the MG.

Her phone rang, and she tugged it out of her back pocket.

"Hi, Wendy." Janey infused her voice with false joy. "Sure, I can talk. Isn't it early hours by you?" Her face paled. "Uh-huh, I understand. So soon? That well? Y-yes, of course. Three weeks? O-okay." She flicked a glance at Max, fear, horror, and disbelief flitting across her brown eyes. "I'm super excited too. Until then, bye."

She dropped her phone onto her lap and broke into great shuddering sobs.

He yanked his seat back as far as it could go, unbuckled her, and tugged her onto his lap. She didn't fight him, instead, melted against him, clinging to his shirt, his arms, anything she could reach.

"I'm so sorry, Max." She sniffed between hiccups. "None of this is your fault."

"Janey, please, I can't help you if you don't tell me what's going on?" He rubbed her back in circles, kissed her temple before nuzzling her hair. The last time he had felt this helpless was when he had held a sobbing Abby the day of their parents' funeral.

"They've moved up the...work event. It's in three weeks, Max. I'm not ready...I can't..." She couldn't breathe, sucking in air too fast for her body to receive it.

Max clasped her face, forcing her to meet his gaze. "Breathe in...and out. In...and out."

She nodded and followed his example. Until she calmed, he cradled her against him.

"We'll double our efforts, find a make-over guru, buy a new wardrobe, anything to give you the confidence boost you need, Janey." He didn't do work functions, but he could rent a tux. "Want me to go with you?"

She shook her head. "I wish. It isn't that sort of event. It's a three-week touring conference."

"Wow." He had never heard of such a thing, not that he moved through business circles. "What do you want our attack strategy to be?"

"Throw everything at this. I'll do the work, Max." She cupped his jaw, running her thumb across his bottom lip, then dipped her head to kiss him.

His heart stilled, then hurried to catch up.

Before he could react, to fully enjoy her soft mouth and addictive flavor, she pulled away. "Thank you for helping me." She scrambled off his lap, touching parts of him that ached for her.

He blinked, stunned. The kiss...if that was what he could call it, was nothing more than a peck. Still, the texture of her lips against his lingered. He flexed his fingers, wanting to yank her back onto his lap.

Instead, he cleared his throat. "Is dinner still on tonight?" He started the engine, letting it idle while they strapped in.

"Of course, one last hoorah. Besides, I promised Abby." Janey leaned back, raised her face to the sunlight, and closed her eyes.

The ride home was in silence, with him swerving all over the roads because he glanced at her too much. Her mood had changed, and she seemed more like herself. Still, he would love to know what the problem was before the phone call, and he sure as hell was dying to ask about Carl.

He bit his tongue until they were on his street. "What did Mr. Beefy want?"

She snorted. "I don't know why you dislike him. He's sweet and adorable."

"You're describing a puppy." He parked in front of the garage and switched off the engine. "You need a strong man, Janey, one that won't take your nonsense or let you sabotage yourself. One that will look after you and want to fuck you all the time."

She gaped, lifting a wide-eyed gaze to his. Her ragged breathing shuddered her breasts. He closed his eyes, wishing he could reach across and feel the tremble through his fingertips.

"You know such a man? Is he on vacation from his oil rig? Or did he fly in after studying polar bears for the whole of my damn life, Max?" She climbed out of his car, but as furious as she was, she closed his door with a gentle touch. Emily would have slammed it with all her might.

"I'm never going to meet him. I hide away from life, from judgment, from new experiences because they...hurt." She bent over the door to grab the shopping bag, flashing a generous amount of cleavage. He trailed her, loving the sway of her ass.

She wasn't in sight when he closed the front door, but Abby leaned her elbows on the kitchen counter.

"What happened?" She dug her hand into Janey's bag, and pulled out a slab of Lindt, a smile blooming across her face.

"Janey received a call that upset her. She asked that we give her space today." He dropped onto the couch, sinking into the cushions as if he didn't have a bone in his body. He accepted the block of chocolate Abby slipped into his hand, nibbling on it in a daze.

He moaned. "I'd forgotten how delicious chocolate is."

"There's a time and place for everything, big brother." She bit into the slab, not bothering to break off a block. "Why don't you tell her how you feel?"

He jerked, the sickly, cloying chocolate coating his tongue made it hard for him to swallow. "What?"

"You were never like this with Emily or any of your clients." Abby sucked on a chocolate-smeared thumb.

"Like w...?"

She clambered off the couch, patting her brother on the head. "You care."

He groaned. Abby was right...he cared, too much, and too fast.

Fuck.

Chapter Fourteen

JANE SAID NO TO Carl. Against Max, he didn't compare. As if she had ever been in a position to choose between two men. She wasn't now, but the thought of stringing Carl along when her heart wasn't free, that wasn't the woman Dad had raised.

After one text to the restaurant to make a reservation, she settled into the chair in front of her laptop.

Stretching her fingers, she started a new document using her manuscript template. Title? Saving Juliet. Series? The Spinsters at Large, book one. On the ride home, with the sunlight bathing her face, she decided to capture her journey. It would be a romantic novel about a plump romance writer, and a fitness instructor named Malcolm Ryan.

Hours passed, and her fingers flew across the keyboard. She drank the iced tea Abby poured for her; ate the health sandwich Max made. A quick Email to her cover designer with the blurb and title would mean a printed book to give to Max before she boarded the plane.

Then he would know who she was, that she'd hidden her identity. Now, it didn't seem to matter. Her shattered, defeated heart no longer cared if he knew the truth or how he would react. Nothing could break her heart further. If it had a crack, a blemish, then yes, but it was in pieces. How could she have been such a fool? The fat girl never got the popular guy.

She whimpered and sniffled as she typed, flicking tears away as if they were a nuisance. Abby hugged her from behind, Max massaged Jane's shoulders while she ate the sandwich, but for most of the day, they left her alone.

The air charged with electricity whenever he entered the study. She sensed where he was, at his desk, fiddling with a camera, and once, watched him from the window as he punched a boxing bag in the studio. He was shirtless, and every movement rippled molten caramel, sweat glistening on each muscular indent.

She added that to the story. On a good day, she could type over ten thousand words. With history and her memories to fall back on, she captured so much detail. Yet, for Malcolm's point of view, she had to see her behavior and interactions with Max from a different perspective. The male character had to react to the female character's words and actions as expected in any type of relationship. This time, in fiction, Malcolm found Juliet adorable, sensual, and utterly irresistible.

Janey stopped to stretch out her fingers, the setting sunlight dimming the room. She had to dress for dinner at six. Saving the document, she closed her laptop, swiveling the chair to smile at Max, having sensed his presence.

"Thank you."

"Feel better?" He scanned her face, assessing her emotional state, no doubt.

"So much better. I'm ready to take this head-on, Max." She pushed out of the chair but paused at the door. "The reservations at six. The dress code is smart casual."

She tucked her head through Abby's doorway. "Abby-babe, what are you wearing tonight?"

She shrugged, sprawled across her bed, a book on her chest. "I have this dress I wear when Max wants to treat me to a fancy dinner." She sat up, tossing the book onto her bed. "Wanna see?"

"Duh." Jane trailed her when she leaped off her bed.

Abby pulled the dress out from the back of her closet. It was too short, too pastel pink, and way too outdated for a teenager. Abby's grimace said she thought so too.

"We need to go shopping." Jane shoved the dress back into the closet. "What if it wasn't dinner with us, but a night at the popular boy's party?"

Abby blushed, pulling out bedazzled black jeans and a gold-silver top.

"Shoes?" Jane draped those items over the bed, placing the black ballet flats on the floor. "Want curls tonight? Maybe a little soft pink lipstick, nothing too over the top."

Playing dress-up with Abby took most of Jane's preparation time. She tugged on the one evening dress she had brought with her, just in case. Dark olive-green fabric crisscrossed her body, from her shoulders to a few inches below her knee, accentuating the fullness of her breasts and hips. In pink-beige strappy stilettos that almost matched her skin tone, she wobbled to the bathroom, brushing, and fluffing her hair. Bold red lipstick followed—the type that needed paint remover to come off. She had chosen this one, so it wouldn't stain glasses, crockery, and men's shirt collars.

After applying concealer around her eye, eyeliner, dark eyeshadow, a little blush, a fresh spritz or two of perfume, she closed the door behind her and headed for the kitchen.

"Wow, Abby, you look amazing." The jeans hugged gentle curves on her youthful body. The shirt highlighted her hair. Gold and silver were wonderful colors on her. "What do you think, Max?"

Janey scanned the room, finding him by the fireplace. Long legs in dark slacks, a navy-blue, button-up shirt, and a black jacket molded to his shoulders. Bouncing blue jelly babies. No matter what he wore, he stole her ability to breathe, like she hadn't had thirty-two years to master it.

"She looks incredible." His voice had thickened as if he was developing laryngitis.

"Max thinks I look older than my age." Abby rolled her eyes.

"Still pretty though. I did say that." He pushed off the mantelpiece and approached, his strides predatorial, his focus not leaving Jane. He circled her, running a hand from her waist to her hip, and squeezed her there.

"Fuck," he leaned in to whisper, his lips brushing her ear. "Wear this to your work function."

Tingles spread from her ear to her harden her nipples. She shivered.

"I love your dress." Abby sucked on a block of chocolate. "Why don't you wear clothes like this, Janey? You wouldn't be single anymore."

"Then evenings out wouldn't be special." She slipped her bank card into Max's jacket pocket, pausing to savor his cologne. She had left her phone on her nightstand. With one more glance at the digital clock, she headed for the front door. "Let's go, we're going to be late."

"Stop." Max's boom froze her so fast Abby collided into her.

"What is it?" Jane stepped between Max and Abby, arching a brow. "Did I forget something?" She patted her breasts and slid her hands down her waist. Everything was in place, no escaping breast, no unsightly lumps.

Max had closed his eyes as if he were in pain with a pulse ticking at his clenched jaw. "I'm the man; I open doors, got it?"

She grinned. "I am man, hear me roar? That's a little chauvinistic. What if I need to pee?"

"Car and restaurant doors." His lips twitched, but he trailed his gaze up and down her body as if he didn't know where to look. "My dad said that opening the door for a woman didn't disparage her worth. He believed it was a sign of respect."

"My dad did the same, but Max, if I reach the door first, wouldn't it be awkward if I stood there waiting? Can't I open the door for you?"

He strode toward her, the gray in his eyes burning with an intensity she couldn't fathom, but her body reacted to it, punching lust into her. She folded her arms across her chest, trying to hide her taut nipples.

He caught her chin with a fingertip and raised it so that her gaze met his. "Then I will reach the door before you, Janey-sweetheart." His focus shifted to her lips, and he licked his as if he yearned to taste her.

"Can we go now?" Abby had the door open, darting in and out as she waited for them.

"Go climb in the car, sport." He hadn't looked away and didn't move or speak until the car door slammed. "I could kiss you now, and it won't be enough."

Jane gaped, and since he had control of her chin, she couldn't hide her reaction.

"You, in this dress, Janey, there are no words to describe how I feel right now." His rough voice, the heat pouring off his body, and the slow sweep of his thumb across her chin said all he needed to say.

"I could change—" She had jeans and a smartish shirt.

"Don't you dare. You look exquisite." He pulled away, laced his fingers through hers, and tugged her toward the door. "Ladies first."

She stepped through, walking to the Audi parked on the driveway. He must have switched cars sometime during the day. The tightness of the dress made walking hard, but helped with the walnut she squeezed between her thighs. Heat, not from the warm evening, pooled in her loins. She ached, she throbbed, she yearned.

Before she reached the passenger door, Max held it open for her. She brushed past him, caught a whiff of his cologne before sliding onto the seat. Holy Moses, who knew Adonis would smell like this? When he was all muscle, sweat, and charm, his scent had been addictive. Did they put pheromones in men's cologne? Mm, she would google that when they got back. The way her body, her senses reacted to his proximity, it felt amplified, as if she had lost her inhibitions. She could fuck him crazy, sideways, upside-down, it didn't matter.

"I'm starving," Abby said from the backseat. "What sort of food does this restaurant make?"

Max slid in, then waited for everyone to strap in before starting the engine. "Where are we going?"

"Casablanca's. Now, Abby, you can eat anything you want. Experience has taught me to either have a starter and a main, or a main and a dessert, not all three. Then again, you're young."

"On the Boulevard?" He pulled onto the road, the soft hum of the car vibrating through the seats.

Jane nodded then remembered neither could see her. "That's the one. Have you two been there before?"

"No, but I have heard of it." He rested his hand on the handbrake, brushing her thigh between changing gears.

Jane couldn't move away from his touch; didn't dare look as if it bothered her. Tonight loomed like the epic cluster fudgesicle this morning was. She had to keep her cool, she had to hide how much she wanted this man, and for the love of all things Moses, he must never find out she loved him.

Chapter Fifteen

OLIVE GREEN, SUCH A hideous color on a house and a motorcycle, but not on Janey. Fuck, seeing her in that dress had exploded desire through his body. Had Abby not been home tonight, Janey wouldn't have left the house.

She didn't need him, didn't need his eating plan or toning exercises. If she dressed like this for her function, she would succeed whatever the goal was.

He still needed her, now more than ever, made worse by this potent lust stripping him bare. Abby looked beautiful, just like Mom. She glowed with confidence, thanks to the attention Janey poured on her. She did it without hidden motives, no trying to seduce Max into a relationship.

Fuck, if only she tried to seduce him.

He shifted in the driver seat, grateful for the tight boy shorts hiding his hard-on. Four months had shrunk to three weeks. He mourned the lost time with her, as if he could continue in good conscience. He would talk to her tomorrow about ending their contract when she stepped onto the plane.

Tonight, he'd pretend they were on a date; that she'd let him peel that dress off, revealing her breasts with her taut nipples. His mouth watered, haunted by the glimpse she gave him through the bathroom door.

"Max?"

He whipped his head to look at her.

"We're here." She cupped his hand holding the handbrake.

Why hadn't he felt her touch? He spun his hand to capture hers, bringing her knuckles to his lips. Her fingers trembled under his kiss.

"Right, dinner. Don't move, either of you." Darting around the hood, he watched them, expecting them to defy his order.

He pulled open Abby's door first, offering her his hand. "Fair Lady Reynolds."

Abby accepted his hand, and climbed out, standing still on the sidewalk. "Good evening, kind sir." She giggled, clasping her hands in front of her.

Max closed her door, and opened Janey's, offering her his hand. "The goddess, Janey Juliet Myerson, temptress, seducer of innocent men, queen of the Sea of Words."

"Oh, well said." Abby applauded, bouncing on her toes.

"Thought you would love that, Abby." Max didn't look at her, his gaze on Janey's face as she stepped out of the car. He didn't back away, instead, he tightened his grip on her fingers, the same hand he had kissed moments ago. Then with a gentle tug, he slipped his arm around her waist, pinning her to him.

"Seducer of innocent men?" Her red lips twitched, and the smile that broke across her face took his breath away.

"Am I not innocent?"

She laughed, shaking her head, cascading her hair around her.

"Have you not tempted me, sweet-Janey?"

She stilled, and the air thickened between them. Her chocolate eyes darkened, promising something delicious. "I do have a degree in breast-juggling, but other than that, alas, my skills on tempting or seducing are greatly exaggerated."

"How do you juggle breasts? Aren't they attached?" Abby gripped her chest, cupping hers then moved her hands up and down.

Max groaned, laughter warring with his need to kiss the woman filling his arms. He ushered them into the restaurant. Yes, he had heard of Casablanca's modeled after the movie. The food was expensive yet worth every penny. The clientele was the bigger concern. Not that he gave a rat's ass whether they photographed him with Janey. That shallow concern had sailed, and he had sent it off with a bottle of champagne, and the middle finger.

What he did fear was if she discovered they had photographed her, and the judgment on social media, what it might do to her self-esteem. That, he wouldn't tolerate. He would monitor the feeds, create search pages, and defend Janey if needed.

He wasn't so famous that people recognized him on the street, but things had a way of leaking. He wasn't ready to share her and hadn't decided yet how to reveal his feelings. With the way his desire steamed ahead, he'd seduce her first then tell her he was in love with her.

His final concern was Emily. This was one of her frequented restaurants with the many "clients" she supposedly wooed for her work. He hadn't wanted to try this place when he might run into her.

"Jane, I am so delighted to see you." A man in a tuxedo rushed forward to greet her. Tall, dark, and handsome in a Mediterranean way, he snatched her from Max, kissing her on her cheeks. "You look wonderful. I have always believed you hid your beauty, and this proves it."

"Giorgio, charming as always." She stood regal, appearing taller, and with a graceful swirl of her hand, she gestured to Max. "This is my fi...Max, and his sister, Abby."

Giorgio gaped. "Any friend of Jane." He kissed Abby but shook the hand Max thrust at him. "I reserved the best table for you, and Luca will be your waiter for the evening."

"How often do you come here?" Max gathered Abby in front of him, letting Janey lead the way.

"Giorgio knew my father." She shrugged, the movement shimmering the dimmed restaurant lighting across her skin.

Max glared at Giorgio when he pulled out Janey's chair. He rushed to pull out a chair for Abby instead. Max tapped the backrest, watching, and waiting for Janey to sit. When she did, he was glad he insisted, because he had a magnificent view of her cleavage.

As the evening progressed, the delicious food and the delicately flavored iced tea he had ordered could not compare to Janey's pink cheeks and frequent laughter. As beautiful as she was, it paled against the friendship she had formed with Abby. His sister glowed, teasing, and laughing as if she had known Janey her whole life.

She'd worn Mom's wedding ring on her thumb and insisted Janey try it on. Ten minutes of badgering ensued, and now the ring sat on Janey's wedding finger.

"Told you I have fat fingers." She held up her hand. The lighting glinted off the marquise-shaped ruby. "We'll need soap to get it off."

"Max will help, right?" Abby wiggled innocent brows, but he wasn't fooled, the minx. She was sending him a message. Shit, he couldn't propose to Janey after five days of knowing her. That was an irresponsible thing to do when his decisions impacted his and Abby's lives.

"Good." Janey sighed, resting her hand on the table.

The ring did look stunning on her—the vibrant color suited her skin tone.

"Hello, Maxy, Abigail." Emily's voice slice through the joyful atmosphere.

He stilled, the air whooshing out of him as ice slithered and coiled around his spine. He hardened his features, not wanting to reveal his hatred, or that she could still invoke it.

He didn't rise, didn't look at her, and wasn't prepared to acknowledge her in any way. Max captured Janey's hand in his, trying to convey he was sorry for whatever his ex-wife said or did. Abby excused herself and headed to the ladies' room. He was happy about that, not wanting another ill-concealed insult to hurt his sister. Emily *was*, as in past tense, his fault, and his problem to deal with. But not anymore.

"Aren't you going to introduce me to your...friend?"

He used to think her girly voice was adorable. Now it grated every nerve she hadn't assassinated during their marriage.

"No."

"I'll check on Abby." Janey rose and sidled past the blonde statuesque woman he'd once thought his type. He watched Janey sashay around the tables, not seeing the admiration men threw at her.

"You can't be serious, Max." Emily folded her arms across her chest. "She's wearing your mother's wedding ring. How long have you known her? You didn't fuck *that* during our marriage, did you?"

Emily looked good in the black cocktail dress revealing large swatches of her skin along with her loose morals. Her hair was longer, dead straight, and her smoky eyeshadow enhanced her blue eyes. She was ice personified, as hard as an ironing board with as much personality.

"None of your business. I don't want to see your face or hear your voice. I won't speak your name. You don't exist."

"Whatever. I expected such childish behavior from you, but to stoop to *that*?"

"She has more personality in her pinkie than you do in your entire body. I adore everything about her, from her breasts to her eyes, and I'd fuck her every damn day if I could. You and I ended when you gave out samples. Who knows what diseases infest you." He curled his lips in disgust. "It's a pity they don't burn an 'A' into women's skin anymore. Every man you fuck needs a warning."

"Did you just call me a scarlet woman?" Emily sputtered, her beautiful face mottling red. He had once thought her exquisite, and he the luckiest man. Now he saw her hideousness, her beauty brittle like a snowflake. One touch shattered her façade, and what lay inside was nothing substantial.

"Is this woman disturbing you, Max?" Giorgio tutted, flicked his fingers, and two burly men removed a screaming Emily from the building. "My apologies. I have watched her do business for many months. It is not good."

"Thank you, Giorgio. I was a fool to marry her. That's on me."

Giorgio gripped Max's hand and thumped him on the back. "We do many stupid things for the illusion of love." He pulled away, nudging his chin at Janey ushering Abby toward them. "She's the real deal, no illusion, all heart and kindness. I would give my life for her." He sniffed, wiped a tear off his cheek, and hurried away.

"What did you say to Giorgio? Was he crying again?" She guided Abby into a chair and hurried after the restaurant owner. By word and deed, she validated the man's words.

"Is Emily gone?" Abby scanned the tables.

"Yes, you missed it. Giorgio had her tossed out of the restaurant."

Abby gaped then giggled. "I hated her, Max. I'm sorry I didn't tell you this before you married her. You looked so happy, I didn't want to ruin it for you."

"You can tell me anything, even if you think it might hurt me." He crouched beside her chair. "Sweet Abby, you're the best thing in my life. Never forget that. I don't regret a moment with you."

"You don't regret it...yet." She lifted the dessert menu but peered at him as he resumed his seat. "If you screw this up with Janey—"

"I've known her for five days." He huffed, lifting the dessert menu just to end the conversation.

"Oh, don't bother reading those. Giorgio is bringing one of each." Janey lowered herself into her chair, her tantalizing citrus scent reaching Max. He fanned the menu card, hoping to breathe in more of her. "He says I've lost weight, and since I'm *engaged*," she tossed a look at Abby, "it's to celebrate."

Platters arrived, along with champagne, and Max had to endure Giorgio kissing him on the cheeks. The man was happy for him, for her, and soon the entire restaurant was aware of this stupendous occasion. He wanted to face-palm, but with Janey and Abby laughing, singing, dancing, and shoving cake into their mouths, their happiness paled against any circumstance he might have to deal with.

Chapter Sixteen

Pain lanced through her skull, piercing it at regular intervals. The constant drone sounded like her phone. Jane lunged for it on her nightstand, nausea roiling in her stomach. How much champagne had she drunk? How much cake? Argh, don't think about the cake.

"Hello?" She buried her face into her pillow, trying to hide from the blinding, debilitating sunlight drenching her room.

"What the hell? Why do I have to hear about your engagement from my hairdresser?" Mom's voice screeched across the connection, and Jane held her phone away from her ear. "You've known him, what, four days? Are you insane? Your father is rolling in his grave, wherever he is."

Pain twisted in her chest, and she shoved her fist into her mouth, then thought better of it. Playing peacemaker no longer interested her.

"Dad rolled over at your first orgy." Heat burned her cheeks at her audacity. "Besides, it was a misunderstanding. I was trying on the ring, and now it won't come off."

"You don't want me at your wedding, do you?" Mom fake-sobbed, a trick Jane was all too familiar with. "Scared I'll trip on your train and flash Max? Daniel ran away like a mama's boy. He wasn't good enough for you, Jane-dear."

She gasped, and a crushing pain squeezed her chest. "You flashed him on purpose?"

"Of course, had to see if he would stay. No stomach, that boy."

Jane jerked, holding the phone in front of her. Her mother droned on, but she no longer listened. With a finger-swipe, she hung up.

"Fudging mother of fudging Moses." She threw her phone onto her bed and stomped to the studio. Ignoring Max who was washing the mats, she kicked the boxing bag, punching and screaming all manner of obscenities.

He wrapped his arms around her waist, and she struggled against the restraint.

"I fucking hate her, have always hated her. I should've told Dad when he first brought Olivia home, but I was four. What did I know?" She crumpled to her knees, taking Max with her. As sobs shattered what little control she had, her tears splattered his clean mats. "I'm sorry." She rocked back and forth. "I'll clean up."

"Fuck the floor, Janey." Max tightened his arms, burying his face in her neck. "Who do you hate? Your mom?"

She laughed, but it was a sad squawk. "Did I tell you about Daniel? How she flashed him, and he ran, never returning my calls? Turns out, she did that on purpose. She broke my heart, not him."

Jane overlapped his arms with hers, snuggling against the warmth of his chest at her back. "She's upset about the engagement and thinks I don't want to invite her to the wedding." She giggled, then snuffed it when she sounded borderline hysterical. "If I ever marry, I'm eloping."

Max kissed her shoulder. "To Iceland."

At that moment, she never loved him more. "Yes."

"Can I bring Abby?" He nuzzled her neck, sending tingles and shivers down her spine. "If we're eloping, I can't leave my sister behind."

"The right woman wouldn't want you to."

He tightened his arms and groaned, the sound vibrating against her neck. "Abby didn't want to go to my wedding, and Emily claimed it would be boring for her. That should've been a red flag."

"You couldn't have known, Max." Jane twisted in his arms to cup his cheek. "Not when no one told you how they felt. One word from Abby might have given you second thoughts."

"I can't pin this on her."

"I'm not saying you should. If Daniel had told me what my mother had done, I might have...we might have..." Her heart wouldn't be lacerated and patched together with chocolate wrappers but in good condition for the man meant for her.

"You're better off without him."

Jane rolled her eyes. "I know that now, Dr. Freud."

He smirked, the curl of his lips sending her heart rate skyrocketing. Please, sweet Moses, let him not notice. "Mm, someone's being a smart ass," she said.

"When have I not been?"

"You're gutsy, sassy, and fearless, as if there's no retribution awaiting you." His eyes narrowed, and his focus lowered, then he moaned, toying with the collar of her...sleep shirt. "I like you in this."

Janey squirmed, trying to break free, and not reveal that she was naked underneath. Tingles skittered along her bare thighs to her nipples, settling in her belly. She had kicked the bag...naked underneath. Remembering a Krav Maga move, she twisted, and slid out of his arms, finding herself on her hands and knees.

He laughed at her, resting his elbows on his raised knees. He was bare from his shorts down to his toes. As she stared at his feet, she had to admit, they were the sexiest she'd ever seen.

"Now what, Ms. Myerson?" He arched a cocky brow, a smirk widening into a grin. When he lunged forward, she didn't see it coming. One moment she was kneeling, the next she was on her back with him crushing her to the mat.

He was warm and deliciously heavy. She didn't dare move. With his thigh between hers, if she shifted, so would her sleep shirt. He pinned her hands by her ears, his smirk back.

"Ha-ha, you win." She tried to lift her hands, but he held firm.

"Have I now?" He leaned down, hovering his mouth an inch above hers. "What have I won, Janey?"

She couldn't breathe, not with the intense gray of his eyes, not with his body acting as a tuning fork. Every part of her quivered and ached for him to...what?

"Aren't you proving a point?" She licked her bottom lip, her mouth as dry as the Sahara.

"What point would that be?" His voice hoarsened, and he shifted, tugging her hands above her head. He captured her wrists with one hand, freeing his other.

She couldn't think, couldn't form a thought, not when he finger-combed her hair away from her face. Not when he toyed with her bottom lip, running his thumb across it, so feather-light she almost didn't feel it.

He dipped his head, his gaze locking with hers, and he came close to kissing her. Nope, no way not with a morning-after breath. She hooked her leg around his, shifted her other foot to rest her heel by his knee, then with one good thrust of her hips, she flipped him diagonally over her shoulder. Once she was free, she bolted, her steps thundering along the Japanese walkway.

Wheezing, she closed her bedroom on a soft click, then laughed. The glimpse she had gotten of Max's stunned face was worth it. Jane sniggered through the shower and managed to slide the wedding ring off with a little conditioner. She pulled on gym clothes, expecting to do something sweat-inducing today, then knocked on Abby's door.

She took the moan as permission to enter.

"Wake up, pumpkin." Jane sat down on the side of her bed, flicking Abby's curls off her face. Her phone buzzed on her nightstand, the same number flickering. "Looks like you're in hot demand. Who's Denver?"

Abby scrambled out of bed, an arm smacking Jane in her bruised eye. She yelped and jumped away.

"So sorry, Janey. I didn't mean to..." The contrition twisting Abby's face had Janey lowering her hand as if her nose didn't burn and her eye didn't water.

She forced a chuckle. "Quit worrying about me, I can use ice. This Denver *needs* you." She ambled out of the room. "Tell me about him later." The moment she passed through the door, she pressed her back to the wall, stretching her mouth in a silent scream of pain. Holy fudgeknuckles, that had hurt.

When Max walked into the kitchen a few minutes later, Jane had a bag of peas on her face, whimpering as she dug in his medicine drawer for pain meds.

"What the fuck happened?" He guided her onto the barstool and pulled out the meds Jane would swear in a court of law hadn't been there a moment ago.

"I hit a wall. Don't ask me how, I'm talented that way. All-natural, the gift from the gods." She sniffled, tasting the salty metallic tang of blood.

"Janey?" He leveled that gray gaze on her, and she was powerless to resist his super-powers.

She muttered something about him being a spy, how lethal his seductive wiles were, and that he could use his intensity instead of truth serum.

"Oh, all right. Abby accidentally smacked me. Please, don't yell at her. She didn't mean to, and it would tear her up if she knew it hurts like fudging fudgesicles." A drop of blood splattered onto the counter. "Um, Max...is my nose bleeding?"

"Fuck." He snatched off the peas and covered her face with a kitchen towel.

"If you pinch my nose, I will kill you." She rolled her eyes at her pathetic threat then groaned as pain lanced her eye. "Peas, please."

"What a lovely lisp you have." He balanced the peas over her eye.

She chuckled, then cleared her throat. "So help me, Max."

"Your threats do not frighten me, Ms. Bond. I look forward to a good spanking."

She giggled and lifted the pea-bag to fake-glare at him. "You say that now, but riding crop burns are the worst." If her face wasn't already on fire, she would be the beacon to warn ships away. How could she explain she knew this from Google, not from experience?

"Why do I always want to kiss you?" That single question, spoken in a perplexed voice, had her lowering the towel, and the pea-bag to blink at him. "Even now with another swollen eye and a bloody nose."

"Do I have to answer that?" What could she say? He needed to get laid, and any woman would do? Hell, she hoped not. She didn't like him 'getting laid' with some Emily-lookalike, but she also didn't want to be the only woman around.

He folded his arms across his chest, pulling his T-shirt tight. "What would you say?"

She grimaced, putting the peas back on her eye. "I'd say you need to find a woman to fuck."

"Then I need to look no further."

Had she thought her eye and nose hurt? Nope, nothing compared to the wrenching pain squeezing the blood from her chest into her head until her face pulsed with her heartbeat.

"No, not me, dumbass. Someone you're attracted to, and not someone who just happens to be in the same room as you."

He didn't respond, and in the continued silence, she lowered the pea-bag to peek at him.

His posture was stiff, and he vibrated with fury. "Is that how shallow you think I am?"

She shook her head and groaned. Nausea, at her situation, and from the waves of pain, coated her throat with bile. "No, you're a man with a broken heart, Max. You fell in love, fell out of love, but what stripped you bare was your illusions of marriage and companionship shattering." She placed the pea-bag on her eye, unable to bear the pain flitting across his face. She' hurt him with her careless words. "You never had either with Emily. For what it's worth, I'm sorry you suffered and that this happened to you." She dropped the bag on top of the bloodied kitchen towel. "You deserve to be happy, and I want that for you, more than anything in this world."

When she squeezed his shoulder, his body was like an ironing board. She smothered a sob. She'd revealed her feelings if he was sensitive enough to pick up on it. As she placed her hand on the passage wall, the dried blood on her fingers was a bold red. With each step, she moved her hand, needing the solid surface to counter her spinning head and stumbling feet. Dizziness assailed her, her face stinging, and spots circled the vision in her good eye. In slow motion, she missed the wall, hitting the floor instead.

Chapter Seventeen

Voices and the stench of sharp antiseptic broke through the darkness. Jane fluttered her good eye open, trying to find her bearings in a turquoise-green room.

"I'm sorry, Mr. Reynolds. I'm afraid we'll have to keep your fiancé until six tonight. Her iron levels were too low for comfort. Her nose isn't broken, but she's re-bruised her black eye. I'd like to monitor her for a few hours." The doctor hesitated. "Tell me again how she became injured."

Did the doctor say fiancé? Jane tried to gather her thoughts and memories. The ring came off in the shower and was in her pocket. Why did her face feel numb? Did she have a stroke when she fainted? Or did she bounce off the floor like a tough-as-nails piñata?

"The first black eye was her trying to stop a mugging." Max looked confident but worried, one hand drawing Abby into a sideways hug. "Today's was because of—"

"I did it. She woke me up, and I punched her by accident. I didn't mean to." Abby burst into tears, burying her face in Max's shirt.

"She's right." Jane croaked, then paused to swallow. "It *was* an accident." She forced a chuckle when she felt far from joyful. "Holy fudgeknuckles, Max, did you teach her self-defense? She has one hell of a left hook."

"Of course. I won't always be there to protect her."

"Hello, I'm Dr. Wolfowitz. How are you feeling?" He tilted her chin to flash a torch in her eyes, although what he would see with her black one, she couldn't say.

"Any relation to Andrea?" Janey mumbled into his sleeve.

He paused. "Why, yes, she's my wife." He withdrew the clipboard. "Please state for the record your full name and the relation to the persons present."

"Um, okay, Jane Juliet Myerson, and he's Maximillian Reynolds, my fiancé. She's his adorable sister, Abigail Reynolds."

Dr. Wolfowitz nodded. "Good, you have excellent memory recall. When were you mugged?"

"Five days ago, I think. You must know my mother, Olivia Myerson?"

The doctor grimaced, his hook nose twitching like a caricature. The tepid lighting reflected off his bald pate, and his eyebrows would beat hers in a contest. Yet he was a lean man with steady hands, and beneath his stern façade, she sensed kindness.

"I'm sorry for whatever my mother said and did. Believe me, it happens often."

He smiled. "Now, let me explain your conditions."

"No need, I overheard you." She blinked at the blood pumping along an IV into her veins. "Transfusion?"

"Yes. Rest, and if you're in pain, just press the button. I'll check on you later." He nodded at Max and left.

"Fiancé?" She groaned, resting her head on the pillow Max rushed forward to plump for her. "I told my mother it was a misunderstanding. I put the wedding ring in my pants pocket." She fondled her hospital gown. "Please dig it out, and take it home. I would hate to lose it here."

"In the panic, I couldn't find your purse. So, I said you were mugged, and that we hadn't received your replacements yet. If I didn't say I was your fiancé, they wouldn't have let us see you."

She nodded, and smiled, hoping to convey she didn't find fault with his decisions.

"Janey, I..." Abby sniffled.

"Come here, sweetheart." Jane gestured to Max to lift Abby onto the bed. As soon she sat beside her, she pulled the gangly teenager into a hug. "I don't blame you. Accidents happen. Look at me. Ask Dumbass-Max how often something has happened to me since he met me?"

Abby raised her hopeful gaze to her brother, who forced a smile.

"It's true. She shoved me into bushes, Abby, and sat on a mugger." Max rubbed her back, and she pulled away from Jane to press her temple to his chest.

"You didn't?" Abby giggled.

"How else was I to stop him? Can you imagine me running after him?" Jane brushed a pale curl off Abby's face, wiping away a tear with her thumb. "So, you see, I don't blame you. I'm made of hardier stuff. Besides, what will happen when you teach me how to box and you black-eye me again?" She tapped her chin as if in deep thought. "I could learn how to throw a tantrum. Got any ideas, Max?"

He chuckled, but his shoulders remained stiff. "Roll on the floor like this morning?"

Jane gaped, not expecting him to flirt. She assumed her face was the colors of the rainbow. Thankfully, when she blushed, he wouldn't see it. "Yes, like this morning, although, I want to upgrade my service. I need a professional tantrum thrower to teach me their ways."

"I can do a little research." Abby raised her hand, missing Janey's face by an inch.

"Right, off you go." Max lifted her off the bed and shoved money into her hands. "Go find a vending machine."

He watched her skip out of the private suite, his face softening. "Thank you."

"For what?" Jane leaned back onto the pillow, careful not to hook the IV. "I meant every word, Max. Accidents happen, and I—"

"No, for your words before you fainted. They were true." His shoulders slumped, pain twisting his features anew.

She rubbed her chest as if she suffered from heartburn. It didn't help ease the heartache, and yet, she was sad she hadn't let their relationship escalate to sex. One night with him would have carried her for years.

She ducked her face, not wanting him to see how he affected her, how he could summon tears with three little words—*They were true.*

"Except for one part, but we'll discuss that when you come home." He cupped her cheek. "How do you feel?"

"Why is my face numb? Am I drooling?" She lifted the collar of the hospital gown to dab her mouth.

"You're not slurring, silly." Max smiled, and this time it filled his face with genuine humor.

"Told you, I'm made of sturdy stuff."

"Sugar, and spice, and all things nice?" His eyes narrowed, and his smile faded. "You scared me, Janey. You do that often. I swear my heart was trying to escape my chest." He finger-combed her hair, gentle when he hit the tangles. "No tennis, no squash, and I'll talk to Bry. We limit your training to the bag. No sparring or hand-to-hand combat."

"Yes, sir, Mr. Bossy Pants."

A nurse came in and injected something into the tube. She smiled at Max but was all professional with Jane. Hello? Flirting with her fake-fiancé in front of her? Not going to happen.

"When's the wedding planner coming over, *sweetheart*?" So, she was jealous, and watching Max smother a laugh was worth revealing it.

"I'll postpone it, Janey-*love*." He kissed her temple and laced his fingers through hers, resting their clasped hands on top of the blankets.

She nodded. He did owe her for Ms. I-don't-have-breasts. She closed her eye, feeling well despite this morning's events. "Do you think that was pain medication she injected into the tube?"

A warm lethargy swept through her, and she snuggled into the blankets. "Truth serum?" She felt as if she lay in the sun on a winter's day. "Amazing drugs."

"I'll let you rest, but I'll pop in every two hours or so."

His voice was distant, and Jane smiled, flicking her fingers in a wave. "Thanks, Max-love."

Chapter Eighteen

MAX-LOVE? WAS SHE PLAYING the fiancé role or did she mean it? He shivered, wishing he could wake her, tell her everything, and beg her to love him.

Instead, he stared at his sleeping fake-fiancé. She looked like she'd done the rounds with Bry on Fight Night. This morning's sparring had left Max hot and hard, and yet, he'd been proud of her when she outsmarted him. Yes, he had blue balls again, but when he saw the bag of peas, all thoughts of fucking her took a backseat to concern.

A bloodied nose didn't stop her from setting him on the straight and narrow, but when she implied she was the only warm body in his radius, fury had torn through him. How could she think so little of herself? Remembering Daniel, he understood why, but to imply Max was so shallow, so sex-driven that any woman would do?

The moment she fainted, his anger evaporated. He carried her to the Audi with Abby sobbing and blaming herself. Janey didn't wake up, not on the ride to the emergency or while they ran tests on her. He paced the waiting room and told whatever lies were needed to stay with her.

Fuck yes, she was his fiancé.

She was mugged, and the judgmental stares accusing him of beating her softened to pity. Abby's constant sobbing added believability to his story, and the nurses ushered them to Janey's bedside.

He still wanted to kiss her. He hadn't lied about that. It might be due to the high levels of lust she inspired in him, he couldn't say. Her words spoke of the damage to his soul. She had seen his agenda, how the sight of her on her picnic blanket had given him hope.

Life was funny, making him believe he wanted one thing, when, if he flipped the coin, there was what he wanted all along.

With Janey, she was both sides to the coin, his salvation. She offered healing for his soul and led him to accept that he couldn't change the past, could only learn from it. He could be the better man, striving to honor his parents in all he did.

He snorted. Yet he had lied to stay beside her. Dad wouldn't judge him for it. "You do what you gotta do, Maxy-my-boy." His voice, with a hint of his father's baritone, echoed in the small private suite he'd organized for her.

Maxy? When Janey said it, he smiled. Anyone else using it tainted his vision red. He would tell her tonight, or at the latest, tomorrow. Perhaps she needed an easy night, watching movies on the couch, then early to bed.

"Is she asleep?" Abby sipped on an iced tea. His had too much sugar in it, but under the circumstances, and with what the vending machine had to offer, he would take his victories where he could.

He nodded, brushing Janey's curls off her temple that didn't need to move. "For now."

"I'm sleeping over at Dev's. You can fetch me from school on Tuesday."

Max frowned. "You know I don't like—"

"You need to tell her, Max." Abby gestured to the door with a nod. "Come, I have to pack."

"But—"

She made a kissy face, scrunching up her lips. "Do you want me there when you kiss her and confess your undying love? I can make popcorn or record it for posterity."

Point made. He grinned. "Fine, Mom." He opened the side table and rummaged through Janey's pants for the ring. She was right, he didn't want to lose it, not when he wanted it on her finger.

"What do you think I should make her for dinner?" He frowned. He didn't know what she liked, what her favorite color, song, book was, yet he wanted to marry her. Max shook his head.

Abby huffed. "Don't even think about not telling her how you feel."

"I wasn't—"

"Sure, you don't know every micro detail, but telling her you love her isn't a marriage proposal. It's an I-want-to-date-you." Abby slurped the last of her iced tea and shook the can.

On the way home, he stopped at the red traffic light, grateful for the opportunity to look at his sister. "When did you get so smart?"

"I got the brains in the family." She raised her chin as if she sniffed manure, then ruined it with a giggle.

"And the looks." He cupped her knee, tears stinging his eyes. "You looked lovely last night, baby sis, just like Mom."

"The light's green, Max." She wiped her eyes, staring at the passing scenery.

Getting Abby home, packed, and delivered to Devon's with a stack of pizza, took most of the two hours. When he arrived at the hospital, Janey slept on. He left the bouquet of bluebells on her side table, kissed her temple, then her lips, and left, promising to return in two hours.

He cleaned the house, did a session of kickboxing, and called Bry with the news. Max was early when he headed to the hospital. Showered, dressed in jeans, and a T-shirt, he held her hand resting on top of the blankets.

"I'd recognize that cologne anywhere." She took a deep breath then fluttered her good eye open. "Hello, Max. Thank you for the lovely flowers."

"How are you feeling?"

Her smile was wide, uninhibited as if she'd consumed too much alcohol and couldn't contain her joy. "Love drugs."

He chuckled but hid it behind a fake cough. "What else do you love?"

"Things I shouldn't." She looked away, staring out of the window. Someone had opened the curtains for her, and late afternoon sunlight poured in.

He didn't want to pressure her when he'd find out soon enough if she loved him back. "Favorite color, song, book, food?"

"Wow, why not have me fill out a questionnaire? Royal purple. Songs? There are too many, and it depends on my mood. For now? Um, Tracy Chapman's Sorry. It's circling in my head." She sat up, and he hurried to plump her pillow. "You?"

"Love Somebody by Maroon 5." The lyrics hit him in his soul, meaning more to him now that he had met Janey.

She nodded. "The music video is inspirational. It's like they're discovering each other." She curled her fingers into his palm, and he tightened his hold. "You found the ring?"

He nodded. "It's in my pocket."

She sighed. "Good. Um, Max, we need to discuss whatever this is. I mean, I'm your client. You shouldn't have to mother me."

She dipped her chin, and he smiled. She was trying not to inconvenience him like he wanted to be anywhere else but here. Oh, Janey. He was about to make a fool of himself, and he couldn't wait.

"Tomorrow is soon enough." He brushed the soft skin of her palm with a stroke of his thumb. "What's your favorite food?"

"Mm, also depending on my mood. Pizza, Chinese, sushi, and I like burgers." She furrowed her brow, then shrugged. "Cheese, chocolate...does coffee count?"

"For a movie night?"

Her mouth parted on an 'oh.' "Sly dog, we're watching movies tonight?"

"If you feel up to it."

"Whatever you make is fine. If it's healthy, that's great too. Three weeks is looming." She gestured to her face. "I hope this heals."

The air thickened with unsaid words and potent emotions that tingled his tongue, urging him to roar from the rooftops.

"You'll look stunning like you did last night, Janey." He tilted her chin and captured her mouth in a sweet kiss he didn't dare deepen. "My color is blue, just like my dad's."

"Blue brings out your eyes." Her breath fanned his lips, and he couldn't smother the shiver in time.

"Oh, excuse me. Dr. Wolfowitz has discharged you early. The test results reveal your iron blood count is up, and there should be no long-lasting effects from your injuries." The nurse moved around the two of them, checking Janey's blood pressure and temperature. She had Max sign a few forms while Janey dressed.

With a hand pressed to Janey's lower back, he escorted her to the Audi. He frowned. He hadn't bought food, thinking he had another two hours to do so. They could pick up something on the way home.

"Hungry?"

Janey grinned, strapping herself in. "I could eat. Let's order in. What will Abby like? Pizza?"

"Abby's staying at her friend's until Tuesday. Her choice."

Silence met his announcement, and Janey's voice was almost too soft for him to hear her. "Is it me?"

"No, never think that, Janey. She decided you needed a little privacy, and she probably thinks I can't handle you *and* her."

Janey laughed. "You'd think she would have more faith in you after all these years."

"She's wise beyond her age. Sometimes I don't know who's the parent in our relationship."

"You raised a wonderful woman, Max. That's something to be proud of." Janey squeezed his forearm.

Fuck, his heart twanged as her compliment slammed into him, juddering his breath. If the fates were watching, he would marry this wonderful woman too.

Chapter Nineteen

"Okay, let's have at this." Jane climbed onto the barstool and waited.

Max had ordered sushi platters for dinner, but the charged tension in the air was almost awkward.

"Now?" He stilled, the light catching the gold in his hair. His pale-gray T-shirt hugged a body worthy of a good licking.

The silence stretched on, her breathing became irregular with her dreading his words. Their relationship was on the cusp of something momentous, but was it friendship or goodbye? Her fingers twitched when she flicked her damp hair out of her face, and she glanced everywhere but at him. Something heavy had pressed on her in the shower as if she had sensed this was ending.

"I know I promised not to leave, but I can go—" Her face throbbed, and her chest rose and fell. She had to calm down. Fainting twice in a day was a new low, even for her.

"Why?" Max cupped her elbows, then feathered his fingers up and down her upper arms.

She shivered, and her nipples tented her dress. Folding her arms across her chest only heightened her reaction. With panic driving her to run, she slid off the stool, prepared to pack. Fudgeknuckles, the way energy coursed through her, she could jog home.

He caught her wrist and yanked her against him. She cried out then struggled, not understanding why he stopped her.

"Fuck, woman, if you keep rubbing yourself against me, I'll take you right here and now."

She stilled, raising a wide-eyed gaze to his face. "What?" As if in slow motion, she shook her head. "Max...I don't understand."

"Right now it is then." He dipped his head to claim her mouth, but she pressed her palms to his chest, keeping him at bay.

"Hold your horses, Mr. Stud Muffin. I didn't pay for this, and I wouldn't in a million years ask you to perform an 'extra' service." She pulled out of his embrace and hurried down the passage, stifling a sob.

As tempting as it was for a night of wild passion, she wouldn't let him. Not only would leaving him in the morning break her heart, but it perpetuated the scarring on his soul. He needed a woman to stay, someone not her.

He stomped along the wood-floor passage behind her and scooped her into his arms. She squealed, clinging to him until he dumped her onto his bed. "I never asked for payment, remember. So, don't mention it again, not when every moment with you has been a joy, Janey."

"What then?" She sprawled across his bed, bare limbs, heaving breasts, peering at him through the tangle of her hair. Huffing didn't clear her vision. "Choose the fat girl and fuck her? Is this a reality show? Some sort of bet?" She whisked her hair out of her face, careful not to punch herself in the eye.

"It's been six days since I met you. Six long endless days of aching for you."

She gaped, running a heated appraisal over his body to the impressive bulge in his jeans. "You're serious?" Her heartbeat roared in her ears, and she sucked in a deep breath, trying to calm it.

"I'm fuck-you-hard serious. In eight days, you're free to leave my home, but there's no way I will tolerate you leaving my life. We're dating. You're my girlfriend, and I don't want to hear no from you."

Put like that, who was she to deny him? Wow, was he for real? Who said stuff like that? Her male characters, that's for sure. Her lips twitched. She let the smile form, unable to hide it, and not wanting to. "It would be nice if you asked."

He placed one knee on the bed, dipping it, then fell across her, catching his weight on his hands. He snatched a kiss, hard enough to sting her lips. "Jane Juliet Myerson, would you consent to date me, to be my girlfriend, to letting me fuck you?"

Her mind reeled while she struggled to process this. "I do declare, you have such a way with words, Mr. Maximillian Reynolds."

"Janey." He nipped her shoulder, her neck, then sucked on her earlobe. She moaned, writhing beneath him, a different ache stealing her senses. "Answer me, please." His need roughened his voice, and his heartbeat thundered under her palm.

"Yes." She embedded her fingers in his hair, scraping his scalp with her nails. "To all of it."

"Right answer, Janey-sweetheart." He captured her mouth, feathering his hands along her ribs, her waist to her hips. He gripped her there, his fingers digging into her as he flicked his tongue, dueling with hers.

She ceased to breathe, didn't care that spots circled her vision. Any nurse at the hospital would agree, a second-fainting from this was worth it. A tug distracted her, and Max yanked, freeing her dress' skirts. He cupped her knee and slid his heated palm along her outer thigh. She squirmed, throwing her arms around his neck, and deepening the kiss.

His hand stilled, kneading as he tilted his head, matching her onslaught and her desire, which had ramped another few notches. He jerked, and broke the kiss, sucking in gulps of air. Amazement or horror morphed his face, but the gray in his eyes swirled, dark, and gorgeous.

"No underwear?" He pressed his temple to hers, his voice rasping.

"It's a house dress."

"I could have, at any moment, lifted your skirts and…" He trembled, his fingers twitching where they now gripped her bare hip. "In the park when I met you?"

She nodded, and he snatched a hard kiss, sliding his fingers over her stomach.

"Max, the sushi—"

"Ten minutes." He feathered kisses along her neck as his seeking fingers brushed across her sex.

Heat, lust, need, love slammed into her, and she moaned, thrusting up to meet his touch. Nothing had ever felt this good. Not even the one time she had sex with Jimmy Barberton in the back seat of his Toyota.

"You're so wet, Janey. Is this for me?" His breath across her ear sent shivers from her neck to her scalp, and he tormented her with his fingers. "Spread your legs wide."

She whimpered, obeying him without thought.

He pulled himself off her to tug one breast free. Air cooled her skin, but when he sucked her nipple into his mouth, she cried out. He groaned and sucked harder, tugging on the sensory cord between her breasts and her sex.

The precipice rushed toward her, and she threw herself off it, powerless to halt the flood of endorphins, the sensations skittering along every nerve and skin cell. She screamed, unable to bear his tongue and fingers.

"You're so beautiful," he whispered between sweet kisses.

She sprawled there, not a solid bone in her body…yet. Everything in her had melted, and she accepted his kisses in a daze. The throbbing tortured her, made worse when he flicked his fingers into her. She moaned, writhing under the sweet intrusion. The ache intensified with each thrust.

"I've waited for this, longed for it, dreamed of it."

"Max, please." She needed another release, needed him in her, stretching her.

"Oh, no, I'm enjoying this, taking it as slow as my control allows." He switched his focus between her lips, her breasts, and his fingers.

She tried to close her legs, tried to take control, but he sucked on a nipple, nipped, and kissed it better. She lost the possibility of forming a thought. He stroked her body, every curve, his touch almost reverent. If she had any doubts about his sincerity, he laid those to rest.

The gate buzzer announced dinner, and he stood, his erection straining his jeans. She rose onto her elbows, delighted that she affected him as he did her.

"Want me to fetch it?" She gestured to his twitching tent.

"Hell, no. I want no one to see you this…aroused. You're mine." He pulled a sweatshirt out of his closet, yanking it on, pulling the hem over his erection. "Be right back, and don't move."

She laughed. "So bossy."

Waiting, she blinked at her bare breast and legs, unable to believe this was happening. She didn't need to pinch herself, not when he'd nipped her enough times to prove she wasn't in an erotic dreamland. She threw herself back, staring at the ceiling, enjoying the hum of desire pulsing through her. Tonight would rock her world like she expected it would. Never had she thought he'd consider dating her. Fudging blue jelly babies, Max was her boyfriend?

The front door slammed, and she rolled off the bed, watching from his bedroom doorway as he slid the containers onto the counter. Grinning, she gathered her skirts and lifted them, baring a hip, and a butt cheek. Her breast hung free as he had left it.

"Want to eat now?" He lifted his head and paused, his attention snagged by her state of semi-undress.

"No, but I do want to know if I should stay like this?" She jiggled her breasts and flashed him her backside. "Or like this?" She whisked the dress over her head.

A growl preceded him bolting down the passage, yanking off and tossing his clothes. When he stopped to toe off his sneakers, she squealed and dove for the bed. He grasped her ankle and tugged until she fell onto her stomach, breathless laughter filling the room. Then he flipped her over, and she swallowed her giggles.

He wore nothing but his unzipped jeans. Soft golden hair feathered across his caramel torso, trailing a path to where his hard-on peeked out.

She gaped, unable to absorb this Adonis before her. "Wow, Max."

He peeled off his jeans, dropping them on the floor. His cock bobbed, and her throat dried.

"Is that for me?" Anticipation was its own aphrodisiac. She couldn't explain the urgency ripping through her muscles, her core, throbbing her with a need he had, but moments ago, satisfied. She licked her lips, rising onto her knees as if to stroke him.

"No, not tonight." He caught her fingers, kissing the tips. "I can't survive you touching me there, Janey. I need you too much."

She nodded. "Tomorrow then." She fell back onto the bed and gestured for him to join her.

He did, sprawling on top of her, nestling his hard-on between her thighs.

She arched when he pressed it at her entrance, promising her more earth-shattering pleasure.

"I'm on the pill," she hurried to say.

He chuckled. "Good to know, and I'm clean."

"Same." She gasped as he pushed into her, too slow to satisfy.

With a smirk curling his lips, he stopped to snatch hot and sweet kisses, doing the opposite of what she needed. She gripped the duvet, digging in her fingers.

"Don't go slow, you've kissed every inch of me."

He leaned back to run his thumb along her seam then sucked on it, closing his eyes on a deep moan. "Not every inch, but tomorrow, I promise."

She shivered, disbelieving he had done that. Sure, she added bits like that in her novels, but she had never had a man do that to her, as if she was the most delicious thing to him.

"Max, please, don't stop fuck—"

"What, Janey? Do you want more?" He slid in farther and halted again.

She cried out, kneading his upper arms, scraping her fingernails down his chest, anything to encourage him to hurry. "More, fast, hard."

"For such an eloquent woman—"

"Max." She reared up and kissed him, conquering his mouth as she longed for him to dominate her. The hair on his chest tormented her but tantalized as well, and she rubbed against him, unable to still her gyrating.

"Fuck." He growled, bending over her to push her back onto the bed. He withdrew and slammed his pelvis forward.

She screamed, the feel of him touching the most sensitive, intimate part of her consumed her focus. She didn't know what she did or said when he pulled out and thrust in again. She rode the wave of emotions, sensations; electricity heightened by her love for him.

Silence descended, a moment amid a sea of energy so intense, that when he withdrew and plunged into her, she shattered. Everything that was Jane Myerson dissolved into particles of pure joy.

He roared, pinning his hips to her thighs as he arched his back, his fingers digging into her hips. "Fucking incredible, Janey, that's what you are."

Warmth filled her, and as she floated down from the sea of ecstasy, she smiled. "You can do that anytime, Mr. Stud Muffin."

He chuckled and sprawled alongside her, twirling a fingertip around her puckered nipple. "I plan to."

In the aftermath of pleasure, awkwardness had her wanting to hide her nudity. Gone was her confidence, her lack of self-awareness. She sat up, glaring at her dress near the door. If she stood up now, he would see all of her without the haze of desire blinding him.

"Don't." He ran his fingers across her stomach to her waist and flipped her to face him. "I adore your body, Janey. Don't hide from me."

"But...Max, I've—"

"Shh, just live each moment with me. Don't overthink this." He snatched a hard kiss, burying his fingers in her hair. He drew away, sucked in a sharp breath, and captured her chin with trembling fingers. "Why do I love kissing you?"

She shrugged, stroking his hip. She could do that now. He'd given her permission to touch him whenever she wanted to. She traced his ribs, then curled her fingers around his shoulders. He shivered, and his nostrils flared. *He likes that, does he?*

"Hungry?"

She nodded, and he rolled away from her, bounding up, then disappeared down the passage. He returned sooner than expected, holding her nightshirt. She didn't care to move, as sweet as the gesture was. She wanted to admire the naked Adonis standing before her. Holy fudgeknuckles, he was gorgeous.

Sorry, J.J. Cox readers, my sex scenes are about to become explicit.

"Janey?" A smile teased his lips.

"Just give me a moment. Don't move." She clambered off the bed and pressed her palm over his heart. "Can I touch you?"

He tilted his head, and nodded, then pulled her into a tight hug. "After you've eaten and taken your pain medication."

"So bossy."

He smacked her backside, and she yelped. "You're so sexy, Janey, and a handful of trouble." He dipped to pick up his jeans and tugged them on. Of all the things she'd thought delectable, watching Max pull on his jeans and nothing else, was drool-worthy.

"Dinner, and something to ogle at?" She gestured to his naked torso, then realized she could touch it. She brushed her fingers through his chest hair.

"Mm, for you maybe." He grinned. "Now hurry, I plan to cuddle with you afterward."

Cuddling? Who was this man? "Just give me a moment."

She grabbed her nightshirt and dress then darted into her room, pulling on a pair of leggings, and nothing else. Catching a glimpse of herself in the bathroom mirror, she blushed. Her face did have the colors of the rainbow, and her nose was a little swollen too.

"Janey?"

"I'm coming, Maxy-darling." She giggled and hurried toward her destiny, no matter how much she might over-analyze this in the morning.

Chapter Twenty

Janey popped a California roll into her mouth, sucking on the chopsticks. She raised her brown gaze to Max's and smiled.

"Fuck," he rasped.

In the soft lighting, her skin glowed, and her nipples were hard, as if the temperature in the room had dipped.

When she came out in her leggings, she clasped her hands in front of her, stricken by shyness. Not that she was aware her actions thrust her bare breasts upward. "Fair's fair," she said.

He didn't taste the sushi, and even though his orgasm had been incredible, addictive, and awe-inspiring, he was still aroused. Fucking her had been everything he dreamed of and more.

"You're sleeping with me tonight, right?"

"I don't know." She tapped her lips with a chopstick, then chuckled. "I'd love to, Max. I've never slept with a man." She leaned across him to dip a roll into the bowl of soya sauce, her breasts brushing his arm.

"Janey?"

She paused in mid-dip, and he snatched a kiss, groaning at her salty flavor. Now he tasted the sushi.

"What?" Her focus shifted to his mouth, lingering there. She put the chopsticks down, cupped his face, and kissed him.

Hugging her trapped her against him. He'd known she'd fill his arms. His body yearned for this, her softness and warmth. He kissed her temple, wishing he could tell her he loved her. She needed that, to know she was worthy. The biggest hurdle was convincing her his attraction to her was real. She still hesitated when she touched him, as if she had no right.

"What do you feel like watching?" He didn't care if it was the Titanic, two hours of watching penguins raise their young, or grass growing on a golf course.

"Let's surf the channels. That way we can learn what the other likes." She pulled out of his arms and planted a kiss on his chin. "First, a shower? You have me on you."

"And you have me in you." He grinned, not minding that at all. She might though. Women were funny when it came to bodily fluids. "Go shower while I'll clean up."

She sashayed down the passage, disappearing into her room. He frowned, then sighed. He wanted her in his shower, pinned to the wall with his cock buried in her. That would have to wait until morning.

He cleared the counter and stored the leftovers in the fridge.

Despite his best efforts to stay away, he leaned his backside on the basin and watched Janey shower. The way her breasts lifted when she washed her hair and her soapy hands lathered her curves, all against her singing Tracy Chapman's Sorry.

He dropped his jeans, and stepped into the shower, pinning her to the wall. There was nothing more wonderful than her sweet lips and the tart flavor of her tongue. He groaned, content to kiss her for hours. Time slowed for him, each movement she made imprinted in his memory. Her kneading fingers, her nails scraping his shoulder blades switching her tongue from teasing to bold. She snatched his breath and rattled his control.

He remembered her sitting on the picnic blanket, so sensual and adorable. Stretching his hamstrings at the bench closer to the lake, he watched her huff, her breasts jiggling. She hadn't ogled him, hadn't even noticed him, and distrusted his motives when he approached her. Her soda bottle tumbling toward him and a J.J. Cox on her blanket had been the opening he needed. Perhaps he'd known then what she'd come to mean to him.

He pulled away.

"I love kissing you too, but at some point, the hot water will run out." She tapped his chest, grabbed the bar of soap, and lathered her hands.

She touched him everywhere, stroking him from his neck to his toes, with special attention to his groin. He was semi-erect and aching by the time she pushed him under the spray of water. When he stepped out, she held a towel for him before drying herself.

In companionable silence, she brushed her damp hair, her towel knotted between her breasts. He took his time to dry off, wrapped his towel around his hips then crowded her to braid her hair.

In her bedroom, under his attentive gaze, she unraveled the towel and pulled on a nightshirt. It felt as if they had been a couple for years, no drama needed. She caught him watching her, laughed, and curled her fingers into the towel to tug him to his bedroom.

"Which closet?" Her focus lowered, and she shuddered. "Holy Moses, Max, I want to taste you." She lunged for the closest door, then the next until she found his stack of sweat pants. She grabbed one and approached him, the brown of her eyes darker. "You said tomorrow, right? Fuck."

"Janey, you said fuck twice today." He chuckled and unwrapped his towel. Her lips parted on a gasp. "You've seen me naked before, but it's never enough, is it?" He grabbed her wrist, and tugged her against him, cupping her backside with both hands.

"You're beautiful, Max, and I'm—"

"Exquisite, sensual, charming, adorable? You best choose one of those, Janey. No one says anything negative about my girlfriend." He kneaded her backside cheeks, then swatted them.

She moaned and arched her back, her eyes closed.

If he didn't step away now, she'd be in pain tomorrow. He wanted her to orgasm a thousand times even if he couldn't. "Want a fire tonight?"

"In the fireplace?" She laughed at his nod. "Pulling out all the stops, Max, when you've already got the girl?"

"Have I?" Max snagged her chin, holding her still for a sweet yet too-enticing kiss. Oh, Janey, how could she not see how much he adored her? Was he in the honeymoon phase of this attraction? Possibly, but he had no doubts that each minute, hour, and day with her would prove she was what she was, the woman of his heart.

He tugged on his sweatpants and ushered her to the lounge. Sinking into the couch, he pulled her down, throwing an arm around her shoulders. She nestled into him, her sigh of contentment echoing in his soul.

While she slept beside him, he dealt with the fall-out from the Casablanca's video hitting his social media feeds. It had gone viral, with most of his fans supportive, others dismissive, and judgmental. Before Janey, he had been the same, assessing people based on their level of self-discipline. He planned to modify his career, helping those who needed him, and not perpetuating the skinny mentality. Ideas circled, and he would run them past Bry. Regular boot camps, nutritionists, check-in buddies all focusing on health rather than weight loss.

Max put his phone down, gathered Janey to him, and inhaled the fragrance of her skin. How the mighty had fallen, and he couldn't be happier.

Chapter Twenty-One

WARMTH SURROUNDED JANE, AS if she floated on a cotton-ball cloud. She snuggled into it, inhaling the addictive Adonis scent. The firm velvet flesh of a man beneath her had her stroking his skin. *Mm, would he look like toffee, taste like it too?*

She fluttered her eyes open and smiled. Max lay on his side, his arm thrown over her, keeping her nose pressed against his chest. She must have fallen asleep on the couch somewhere between a reality show and a documentary.

She shifted, rubbing her belly across something hard. This was tomorrow, and before she could talk herself out of it, she stroked him from balls to tip. He groaned in his sleep, pulling away to sprawl. Perfect.

She rose onto her knees, and opened her mouth, sucking him in as hard as he had tormented her nipples. Then she licked his head, and the shaft while caressing his balls. She didn't look at him, not when she sensed he had woken up, not when he slipped two fingers between her thighs. She lapped and sucked on the caramel length of him like she was on death row, and he was her last toffee.

"Janey, no fair."

She twisted to watch him as she scraped her teeth over his head, as light as she could, not wanting to hurt him. His balls tightened, and his cock bobbed. He arched off the bed, his fingers stilling where he flicked her nub. "That feels..."

She sucked hard, pulling him deep into her mouth, tearing a growl from him.

He tugged her off him and flipped her over. "No, I'm not coming like that. I want in you, I want you gushing around me, I want to *feel* you orgasm."

She laughed. "I want that too, but Max, I enjoyed that..." She licked her lips, moaning at the masculine savory taste of him.

Instead of plunging into her, he spread her thighs wide, dipping to run his tongue along her inner folds.

She gasped, her teasing evaporated.

He groaned, widened his mouth, adding more pressure with the tip of his tongue. He slid a finger or two into her as he sucked on her clit. All thoughts, hopes, and dreams evaporated under the onslaught. She could only feel, ride whatever sensational rollercoaster he had her on. She stilled, she shuddered, she moaned, and writhed.

"Max," she panted. "Please, don't stop."

Then he curled his fingers, hitting her G-spot. She exploded, unable to hold back the dam of pleasure tingling her nipples, and quivering her belly. He nipped her inner thigh, rose onto his knees, raised her legs to his chest, and thrust in.

She arched off the bed. His intrusion was too close to her orgasm with every inch of her sensitive, charged, and flushed with endorphins.

She came again but he didn't grant her mercy, thrusting, withdrawing, hard, fast, slow until she lost count of how many times she saw stars or screamed his name. Then he stilled, his eyes rolling back, his body spasming, and he grunted.

He opened his eyes and brushed a damp curl off her temple. A slow, satisfied smile sauntered across his lips, and the gray in his eyes softened. He spread her thighs, layered his body over hers, and rolled them. He was gentle when he positioned her limbs across him.

"Good morning, my girlfriend." He stroked her hip and kissed the crown of her head.

"Good morning, my boyfriend." She dipped a fingertip into his belly button and swirled patterns around it.

"How do you feel? In pain? Hungry?"

"I'm happy, Max." She rose to look at him when his fingers stilled. Had she said something wrong? She diverted her gaze and spotted her Lone Rider on his nightstand. Fudge, she would need to tell him that she had lied to him, that she wasn't who he thought she was. She pinched her lips, wishing she didn't have to; that she could enjoy another day with him.

Therein lay her problem, she loved him, and each moment she spent with him, the more in love she fell. If she waited, it would worsen her broken heart. If she told him now, he might forgive her, might let her stay.

She was a pathetic spinster grateful for a morsel from heaven. Tears prickled behind her eyes, and she rolled across the bed until she sat on the edge. "I have to tell you something."

"What is it?" He hugged her from behind, bringing his strength, his warmth, and making it harder for her to speak.

"I'm so scared that if I don't tell you now, you'll hate me, and if I wait, I'll fall more in love with you. I..." She sniffled then sucked in a deep breath, taking the plunge. "My dad called me JayJay, Max." She kept her gaze down, not wanting to see his anger, or worse, his hatred. She had deceived him for over a week.

"Makes sense, Jane Juliet."

She laugh-cried, dashing the tears away from her good eye. "My birth mom's maiden name was Cox." The tears streamed down like they had broken the banks. There was no stopping them until they had run their course. "I'm sorry. I don't tell anyonne my pseudonym." She sobbed, folding her arms across her chest. "I planned on not sharing this with you since we had a business contract. After four months, you wouldn't see me again." She slumped her shoulders, pinning her trembling hands between her thighs.

"Wait, back up." He gripped her shoulders and twisted her to face him. There wasn't hatred on his face, no disdain, no judgment. He gaped at her, his eyes wide in awe. "You're in love with me?"

She gasped, slapping her hand across her mouth. "I said that? I didn't mean to, not so soon, not until..." She raised her face to the ceiling, trying to breathe past her blocked nose. She'd fudged this up. Typical, just like Daniel, Max would run, or in this case, chase her out of his life.

She laughed, not caring if she was hysterical. Their relationship had escalated to sex, and like she thought would happen, she had memories to carry her through the lonely years ahead. That was all she was worthy of.

He stared at her with the softest expression then cupped her cheek, running the pad of his thumb across, wiping her tears. "I'm in love with you, Janey."

She clutched her chest, unable to silence her pounding heart or the feeling that time had slowed. "What?"

"You've just told me, the woman whose words I've jerked off to for the past four years is the woman I'm in love with? You think I'm upset about that?"

"You love me because I'm J.J. Cox?" She frowned, darkness coating her heart, the pain like a joy-sucking black void. This was worse than his hatred.

He growled and grabbed the book, shaking out the laminated card she must have left inside it.

She snatched it off the crumpled sheet and pressed it to her lips.

He swiped the card from her and pointed to the reader's name. "How do you feel about this man?"

"I adore his reviews and can't wait for them, to be honest." She smiled at memories of her squealing when he'd post something then walking on euphoria for days afterward.

"Would you love me more or less if you knew I'm ArdentMan?"

She switched her gaze between the card and him. What? She shook her head, trying to dislodge the haze of disbelief.

"Would it make any difference here?" He pressed his palm over her heart.

"No." She didn't believe him. What were the odds of running into her biggest fan? Astronomical.

"Then why would you think it makes a difference to me who you write as?" He dropped the card and grabbed his phone, typing something with his thumbs. Her phone dinged, and she reached for it in slow motion. There on Amazon sat a new review, five stars.

 ArdentMan

☆☆☆☆☆ Ask me about the video, my love.
Reviewed on July 13, 2020
Verified Purchase

You're exquisite, sensual, charming, adorable.
I love you, J.J. XOXO

Stunned, she gaped at him, finding him holding out his phone. An fan-posted video played of him talking to Emily, confessing his adoration for Jane.

"I loved you before you told me, Janey."

Trembles assailed her. Warmth soaked every pore. She'd never been this happy, but happiness was fleeting, untrustworthy. She bit her fist, tears running anew. "Really? I can keep you?"

He hugged her, crushing her within his embrace. "Oh, sweetheart." He held her for a while, whispering when and how he'd fallen for her. He leaned back, tilting his head. "This three-week conference isn't a book tour, is it?"

She nodded, her looming trip snatching a little of her joy. "I don't want to go, and now that I've found you, I'm dreading it even more."

"Janey, this is for your readers. You have to go." He brushed her hair off her face, his touch gentle.

She nodded. "I know, and it's in my contract." She pressed her palm over his heart. "What will Abby say about us?"

"Why do you think she's not here? She told me she's leaving us alone so I could get off my backside and confess my undying love. Her words."

Jane laughed, too happy to contain it. "I love your sister."

"Good, you have the package deal, Ms. Janey Juliet Myerson J.J. Cox."

Epilogue

A LOT HAD HAPPENED, all good. Jane kicked her mom off the property and put the house up for sale. That had been an argument she'd enjoyed. She wasn't one for confrontation, but the shock on Olivia's face was now a cherished memory. A company packed Jane's belongings, and when she found her forever home she would move in. What she wanted most was for Max and Abby to ask her to stay with them. The last time she had been this happy was when Dad was still alive.

Max had become her beta-reader, brain-stormer, and role-playing (nudge nudge wink wink) go-to. He added grittiness to her sex scenes when she wrote from the male character's perspective. He had remodeled the guest bedroom so that she had her own office. Through no fault of her own, she distracted him with muttering, sobbing, and sighing. Her new mechanical keyboard meant he couldn't record his fitness videos.

As to the contract, they agreed to invest her four-month payment into a trust fund for Abby. Perhaps it could be for a trip abroad when she was older.

Like Jane's book tour? Tears stung the back of her eyes. This was goodbye, well, for three weeks. No kisses, no mind-blowing sex, just work. She placed her laptop beside her bag then faced the mirror one last time. She'd lost seven pounds, which Max was ecstatic about. He adored her curves and had demonstrated his obsession over the last three weeks, erasing all self-doubt.

Her leggings and draped blouse suited her, adding mystery and sensuality to her shape. Her wardrobe had undergone a drastic remodeling, except her day dresses. Max loved catching her unaware for a quick fondle.

Jane sniffled, tears shimmering on her mascaraed eyelashes. She patted a fingertip around her make-up, trying not to ruin it. As the departure date drew near, she slept less each night, wrote more. Max had tried to make her rest, but she couldn't, dreading the upcoming trip, as always.

"Ready?"

"Max," she rasped. She struggled to breathe, her chest too tight. A tear escaped, and she flicked it off her cheek. She wouldn't ruin one of the last glimpses of her boyfriend with an ugly cry.

"Oh, Janey." He hugged her, his strength, his love pouring into her with that simple gesture.

Burying her nose into the curve of his neck, she inhaled his cologne, trying to trap it in her lungs. Blue jelly babies, how she loved this man.

"Dumbass, tell her." Abby leaned her backside against the door, folding her arms across her chest.

He laughed, and Jane glared. Here she was, miserable, and he had a stupid fudging grin on his face. He gathered her luggage ignoring the questioning lift of her brow. Abby grabbed her hand and tugged her into the lounge. She released Jane and hurried to the door bouncing up and down, as if she were a puppy proud of having wet the rug. By the front door stood luggage but not Jane's.

"What's this?" Her heart fluttered, and she cupped her mouth, not wanting to hope, but unable to stop herself. "Max? Abby?"

He stood there, jeans molding his thighs and tight ass. A plain navy T-shirt clung to muscles she had licked every inch of, and the one stray sunray that followed him shone upon his golden hair. Her Adonis, her Gabriel. He looked worried, as if he had done something, and feared her reaction.

He'd worn the same expression when he surprised her by moving Dad's piano into his home. Every time Abby tinkled with the keys, Jane cried, as if her father had returned. She stopped, whatever she was doing, to listen.

"We're coming with you." Abby threw her arms around Jane with too much enthusiasm, crushing the breath out of her.

Jane focused on Max, waiting for him to confirm it. She wouldn't let the champagne-like excitement free until then.

He grinned, sauntered toward her, and hugged her and Abby, brushing his lips across Jane's ear. "It's true." He stepped back and nodded at Abby, who skipped away to wheel the luggage to the car.

Max clasped Jane's hand, lifting her fingers to his lips. "I love you more today than I did twenty-three days ago. It's why I asked Wendy to help. Abby and I will be there for you every day, Janey, and if you don't think it too presumptuous of me, I'd love to end the trip in Iceland."

All right fudging tears, leak, dammit. She couldn't stop them, couldn't speak without sounding like an asphyxiating cat. She nodded, feeling as if her heart might explode. Excitement set her senses on fire, her skin tingling, while a stray breeze whipped her hair. For the first time since that fateful day at the park, she looked forward to the trip.

He knelt and held up his mother's wedding ring, pinched between forefinger and thumb. "And...," he drew in a deep breath, a tremulous smile teasing his lips, "...marry me, Janey, be my forever."

Her mind reeled, and her vision swirled in the opposite direction. Mother of Moses, not again. She dropped to the floor, but instead of collapsing, she threw her arms around him, nodding like a bobblehead. She couldn't speak, just blubbered like the walrus she used to be.

He laughed, crushing her to him. She melted into him, accepting that he'd always be her home.

He kissed her temple, her nose, then pressed his lips to hers. "You need to say it, Janey-sweetheart." His breath fanned her lips, and she shivered, drowning in the turbulent gray of his gaze.

"It's a fuck yes, Max."

"Language." Abby laughed from the front door, recording them with her phone. "Can we get chocolate at the airport? You two have made me emotional."

"Just like that, the moment's gone." He rolled his eyes then snatched what breath Jane had left. He kissed her hard and long, ignoring Abby's huffs of impatience. With his tongue and lips, he teased and tormented Jane until lust coiled—heated and expectant. "Shall we, my Rubenesque goddess?"

She answered by slipping her hand into his.

About the Author

Sevannah Storm is a fiction writer who immerses herself in fantastical worlds both magical and science fiction. She has a flare for the creative, having studied art and interior architecture, and spends her time drawing, oil painting, and writing. An avid reader from an early age, Sevannah finds her inspiration from various sources: games, novels, music, and the land of make-believe. The unique versus the practical has brought on numerous debates.

In her spare time, she does Pilates and rereads novels that snatch her breath away. Having embraced the social media world, you can find her on most platforms.

Her home is a land south of Wakanda, where animals roam free. Born in Zimbabwe, she grew up in South Africa. The crisp blue skies with cotton-candy sunsets expand her heart and soul, encapsulating a sense of freedom.

Words she lives by: "Know your pothole and dodge it. Don't work in a pencil factory if you're a vampire."

Sevannah loves to hear from her readers. You can find and connect with her at the links below.

Website/Newsletter:

https://www.sevannahstorm.com/

Facebook:

https://www.facebook.com/sevannah.storm

Instagram:

https://www.instagram.com/sevannah.storm/

Twitter:

https://twitter.com/sevannah_storm

Thank you for taking the time to read *Plump Jane*. If you enjoyed the story, please tell your friends and leave a review. Reviews support authors and ensure they continue to bring readers books to love and enjoy.

www.ingramcontent.com/pod-product-compliance
Lightning Source LLC
Chambersburg PA
CBHW070312120726
47910CB00007B/2453